the sadness of spirits

BLUE LIGHT BOOKS

The Sadness of Spirits

stories

Aimee Pogson

INDIANA UNIVERSITY PRESS
INDIANA REVIEW

BLUE LIGHT BOOKS

This book is a publication of

Indiana University Press
Office of Scholarly Publishing
Herman B Wells Library 350
1320 East 10th Street
Bloomington, Indiana 47405 USA
iupress.indiana.edu

Indiana Review
Bloomington, Indiana

*Manufactured in the
United States of America*

Cataloging information is available
from the Library of Congress.

ISBN 978-0-253-05045-8 (paperback)
ISBN 978-0-253-05046-5 (ebook)

1 2 3 4 5   25 24 23 22 21 20

Versions of these stories have been
published in the following journals:
"Unnatural" in the *Berkeley Fiction Review*,
"Red Ballooning" in *Juked*, "Oh, Dr. Brown"
in *PANK*, "The Long Man" in *Western
Humanities Review*, "Uncle Rumpelstiltskin
Will Teach You to Dance" in *Chautauqua*,
"The Sadness of Spirits" in *SmokeLong
Quarterly*, and "These Clouds, These Trees,
These Fish of the Sea" (as "Cooking for
the Emotionally Repressed") in *Nimrod*.

For Kevin, Every Day

contents

acknowledgments

It would be impossible to list all of the people who supported me in the creation of this book, but I will do my very best.

First, thank you to the *Indiana Review* staff for seeing the potential in my work and being willing to give it a chance. I'm grateful that my first book found such a great home.

Thank you to the many people who have helped this book along its journey at Indiana University Press. In particular, thank you to Ashley Runyon, Anna Francis, and Leigh McLennon for their insight and their patience with my many questions.

Thank you to my fellow MFA students Dustin Hoffman, Brandon Jennings, Angela Purdy, Joe Celizic, Brad Modlin, and Megan Ayers for their feedback and friendship. Our conversations both in and out of the classroom have stayed with me for all these years.

Thank you to my professors at Bowling Green State University: Lawrence Coates and Wendell Mayo. They allowed me to be contrary in the best way.

Thank you to the friends who have constantly encouraged and believed in me, including Allison Pavolko, Stacy Malena, Elizabeth Fogle, Sharon Gallagher, and Celise Schneider-Rickrode. Thank you to Mara Taylor for being the very best writing partner and for keeping me focused. Thank you to my very talented writing group—Joshua Shaw, Evan Ringle, George Looney, and Tom Noyes—for their feedback and support. Thank you especially to George Looney and Tom Noyes for guiding me through this process of becoming a writer for so many years.

Thank you to my parents, Rick and Theresa, who have believed in me since I first started writing stories in my notebook so long ago. Thank you to my sister, Erica, for listening to me talk about those stories.

And finally, thank you to Kevin for always being my first and best reader.

the sadness of spirits

Unnatural

I awoke this morning to find a dead salmon lying outside my bedroom window, its vacant black eyes rolled upward, reflecting the summer sun. This is the fifth such salmon I have encountered this week. I promptly removed it from my windowsill, wrapped it in newspaper, and put it in the freezer. I have never really known how to dispose of salmon, and so I stack them in my freezer, to be dealt with another day.

I brew a pot of coffee and consider this influx of dead fish. I find them everywhere: in my car, on my doorstep, inside my closet, tucked in my shoes. I am neither a fisherman nor an ocean dweller. There is no reason for these salmon to invade my house; I did not invite them.

I look for a river, a stream, a series of puddles a salmon can jump through, but I find nothing.

The children sit on a fluffy carpet in front of the TV, mesmerized by the were-man in the swamp. I don't know why the other preschool teachers insist on showing the children this movie; it will certainly give them nightmares. I like seeing the kids quiet, though. It gives me a chance to study them, to imagine their futures, the people they will become.

There is one girl in particular who reminds me of myself when I was young—or at least the way I like to remember myself. Her hair is dark and wavy, her eyes curious and green. She follows directions with enthusiasm and giggles over macaroni creatures and the boys' endless antics. I watch her as she watches the were-man—the tense tilt of her head as she follows his motions—and remember when I was young, innocently watching TV, doing whatever my teachers told me to do, packed into a small room with other kids whom I would never choose to befriend in another ten to twenty years. When I look at this image of my other, younger self, it is hard to see the resemblances between the child and the woman I have become.

I sigh and open my desk drawer to find a tissue. I find myself face-to-face with a salmon.

I once held hands with a man who worked in the seafood section of a grocery store. The scent of scallops and shrimp hung on his fingers. I imagined microscopic bits of scales caught under his nails, remnants of a life lived at sea.

I held hands with him again and then again. His eyes were murky. His voice lured me into something dark and oppressive. When I closed my eyes, I felt myself descending. I thought, *This is what it means to drown.* I found a man who wore expensive cologne and kissed him long and hard.

Salmon bodies appear in my bathtub as if lured by the prospect of an eventual bath. I scoop them out, carry them to my freezer. I am running out of room.

I have decided to seduce a sushi chef. My freezer is full, and I have no other options. I cruise past the sushi counter at the grocery store, batting my mascara-laden lashes, smiling in the chef's general direction.

I walk by again and again until his eyes begin to follow me, then I make my move. I approach the counter, look into his eyes, and say, "I will take a tuna roll."

"Tuna," he repeats. "That's a good choice."

I smile and nod. "Yes, it is," I say. "Indeed, it is."

The were-man is on the move again. The children watch him with anxious eyes, flinching as he attacks various woodland creatures. I look at the other teachers, and they smile and nod. Clearly this is educational somehow.

I watch the dark-haired girl and wonder whom she will grow up to love. I imagine the ways her life will be shaped and bent by others.

Sometimes I place myself in the position of this girl, frightened by the were-man, eager to go home and play video games or run around outside. Her life stretches before her, seemingly endless, punctuated by certain turning points: high school, college, marriage, a career. She doesn't understand that these events are just small segments of her life. She doesn't understand the vacancy in between, the endless day-to-day reality that needs to be confronted. She doesn't see the details, the lines and color and clarity and flaws that real life presents. A plan is a plan, but plans often get changed. Directions alter. Others get in the way. Sense and order and logic can be smashed, disrupted, and overturned. Love is love, but love is also fear and trust and distrust. It is connection and disconnection, friendship and desertion.

For me, love was a man who woke up grumpy, calmed after coffee, laughed often, and never remembered to return phone calls. He turned the world upside down in a way that was beautifully devastating, uniquely wonderful. I held my breath when he told a joke, anticipating his amused smile more than the punch line. I held his hand while he watched TV, a book balanced in my other hand. I felt vulnerable in his presence, in a way that was both pleasant and terrifying. I ventured into him, the mystery that is another person, and he ventured into me, uncovering, exposing. It is possible to snap under such scrutiny, to cringe as your own flaws and secrets are recognized, one by one. It is possible to distrust and disconnect. This kind of intensity makes you consider the front door, the way the hinges always creak like the wail of the dead and opt instead for an open window as you make your escape one late spring night.

I couldn't have known this when I was young, but life is hard and frightening. All of it, without exception, from beginning to end.

The sushi chef sits at my kitchen table eating a spicy stir-fry that I have spent the better part of the afternoon laboring over, finding the recipe, shopping for just the right ingredients. I watch as his face flushes from the hot peppers and the endorphins I imagine must be racing through his body. I make small talk and tell him jokes. I describe the preschool where I work, occasionally glancing nervously at the salmon that has appeared on my bookshelf. After dinner, I lead the sushi chef to my couch, put in a movie, and slowly edge closer and closer to him until we are sitting shoulder to shoulder, hip to hip. A few minutes later we are kissing, wrapped in an embrace that is strange simply because we are strangers. I think of the salmon stacked in my freezer, of the man who forgot to return phone calls, and it occurs to me that I shouldn't be doing what I'm doing. I should feel guilt, shame, a strong sense of self-contempt, but instead I am vacuous. I am hollow. I am a shell. I am a woman who is running out of room in her freezer and has no other options.

A little while later, I lead the sushi chef back into the kitchen and make him a cup of coffee, dark roast, my specialty. While we are waiting for the coffee to brew, I casually open the freezer and offer him some salmon. "My brother loves to fish," I lie. "And he's always stocking my freezer. Why don't you take some?"

The sushi chef smiles awkwardly and leaves with two, and only two, salmon. After he is gone, I take the rest of the coffee into the living room and recline on the couch. I study the salmon on the bookshelf, its pinkish red scales so similar to my own flushed skin, and imagine the way blood and veins flow scarlet and cross our bodies. There are so many colors that demonstrate life—green and red and brown and gold—but when I close my eyes and picture myself as I feel, I see only a scattering of gray.

I am at the bank, depositing a check, when I notice that the teller is wearing a wedding band. I casually let my eyes wander up to his face, verifying what I had only half noticed before. The teller appears to be very young, barely out of high school. His face is boyish and smooth; his blond hair is a mop of curls. He is at least fifteen years younger than me, but judging by his job, his dress shirt and tie and wedding ring, he is clearly more settled. I imagine him marrying his high school sweetheart, adopting a dog, having a child, embracing a career in the same town he lived in his whole life. I wonder if this is the way things are supposed to be. I wonder if there is something terribly wrong with me.

I am distracted when I reach into my purse for my checkbook and don't notice the difference between scales and the smooth, lined cover of my checkbook. When I remove my hand, I am holding a salmon, its dull dead eyes staring helplessly at the teller. The teller gazes at the salmon and then slowly looks at me. "Is that natural?" he asks.

I shake my head, unsure. It occurs to me that I am a woman who breaks hearts and scares children; I don't know what natural is. I think back on the events of my life and wonder if I have done everything wrong, taken all the wrong turns, made bad decision after bad decision. I don't even know because I can't see myself clearly. I feel my way through life from a blind place inside myself. "I don't think so," I say finally. "But what can you do? They keep showing up."

The teller shrugs and shakes his head. As I am leaving, I see him cast a sympathetic glance in my direction.

The sushi chef and I are lying in my bed. Somehow he has ended up with my pillow, and so I lay my head against his arm and try to ignore the discomfort. He turns to look at me and says, "I love you."

I don't know if he is in love with me, the intimacy we have shared, or the salmon I send home with him each time we meet, but really, I'm too tired to think about it. Instead I say the first words that come to mind, "Don't love me. I can never love you."

He turns to look at me, too dumbfounded to speak, and for a moment we lie together in silence. I wonder if I am the first woman to resist his declarations of love, to turn down an offer of romance in a world where everyone is looking for a soul mate. I expect him to roll out of bed and leave, maybe add a smart remark or two, but he only sighs and says, "Sometimes I can't believe you work with children."

"What's that supposed to mean?" Random cruelty I can deal with, but a personal attack? I didn't even think we knew each other well enough for that.

"You're just so high-strung." He strokes my hair like I'm a puppy or a beloved cat. "You need to relax a little. Have fun."

I try to remember the last time I had fun, but all I can think of are the salmon that keep showing up around my house. On my windowsill. In my dishwasher. Under my bath towels. The salmon are wearing me out. I'm tired of wrapping them in newspaper, trying to think of ways to dispose of them.

"You know what I do when I'm stressed out?" he says. "I imagine that I'm in my favorite place. I close my eyes, breathe deeply, and try to remember all of the details. You have to think about what the place smells and sounds like. You have to make it as real as possible."

"That's nice," I say. I can't imagine ever taking the time to mentally transport myself to a "favorite place," but I try to sound enthusiastic.

"Why don't you try it now? Just lie back and imagine your place. I'll do it, too." And just like that his eyes are closed and he's gone, breathing in and out, experiencing his happy place.

I stare up at the ceiling for a moment and then close my eyes. I'm not sure what my favorite place is. When I try to think of a favorite place, I draw a blank. When I think harder, I come up with a series of generic places—my grandma's kitchen, my childhood backyard in winter, the mall—none of them places I am really attached to. I finally settle for a field, a meadow of sorts. I have been in a meadow only once or twice in my life, but it seems like a satisfactory favorite place, quiet, far away from people and salmon.

I imagine that I am standing in the center of the meadow.

I imagine that there is a slight breeze, making the tall grass wave like it is being stirred by a million tiny fingers. There are flowers, too, purple flowers. Purple is my favorite color. Flowers are some of my favorite objects. I stop to smell them in the grocery store.

I try to imagine myself breathing in and breathing out, but I can't. My chest feels tight, constricted. I gasp for air, but nothing comes. I am standing in open air, and I am drowning. On the ground before me is a salmon, its mouth opening and closing easily. I open my eyes with a start, relieved to be back in the bedroom.

The sushi chef turns to look at me. "Are you okay?"

I nod, unable to speak. He continues to watch me, his eyes dark and worried. "Most people don't react that way to their favorite place," he says. "What were you thinking about?"

"Nothing," I say. "I'm fine." I feel dissected by his gaze, my actions turned over and prodded, and I look away. He runs his hand along my arm, waiting for me to speak, and I feel a shiver of longing, cold and frightening in its need. When he leaves later that night, I will stretch myself across the bed, taking all the space for myself. I will stop returning his phone calls. I will erase him from my mind. For now, I fix my attention on the far wall and shrug off his questions.

The salmon will continue to appear, in plant holders and under pillows, a migration running directly through my house, crowding my space.

When the were-man devours a rabbit, bones snapping and cracking, several of the children reach their breaking point. There are gasps, sobs. The dark-haired girl gets up and tries to run out of the room, crying, and I am the first to intercept her. I get down on one knee, bringing myself to her level, and try to envelop her in a hug. A hug seems reasonable to me, especially after the sight of such a brutal and untimely death, but she pulls away, runs to another teacher who has come up behind me. As the other teacher comforts her, the dark-haired girl gives me a funny look from beneath her tears. "You smell," she tells me. "Like fish."

I take the were-man movie home with me and watch it once, twice, studying the furry man in the swamp, hunched and filthy, preying on small defenseless creatures. As I watch, I wonder who the man was before he became the were-man in the swamp. Was he married? Did he have children, a job, responsibilities? Or was he someone who always hovered on the edge of humanity, unable to connect, waiting for that one bad day that would send him running into the wilderness?

I wonder what I am meant to take away from this film and why we are showing it to children. I think about the line between the carnal and the civilized. When I close my eyes, I see the man who never returned phone calls. I see his hands, the freckles that dotted them. I feel the rough patches of skin at the tip of each finger, along each knuckle. I sense the way love can be endless, deep, consuming, terrifying, and the way he embraced that love, expecting me to do the same. Then I remember jumping from the bedroom window, spraining my ankle, and dragging myself on despite the pain.

Am I supposed to understand the were-man, or am I supposed to fear him, to be afraid of ending up like him?

There is a salmon on the coffee table, reclining beside the candy dish. For a moment, I consider touching the salmon, running my fingers along its scales, looking into its empty eyes. So many salmon and I haven't truly touched a single one. I lean forward until I can see each individual scale, the patterns of color. I reach out my hand, straining toward the salmon, and then stop, unable to bring myself to touch the fish. I lean back against the couch, study the salmon, and wonder how much longer this will go on.

Red Ballooning

I don't know where to start, but I love him, and so I slice off my ear. There is nothing more true to ecstasy—all those starry, starry nights—than an ear wrapped in tissue paper, tucked in a box, and sent through the US mail.

If it fits, it ships. He'll receive it in exactly three to five days.

Balance comes from the ears but also from something deeper, because I was often unbalanced before I met him, and I'm unbalanced now but also very, very balanced. So balanced it's like I'm standing straight on a trampoline with a tray of red wine while everyone else flies off in chaotic directions. It's like I'm in a flat land with flat people, and everyone is talking in whispers, and I'm there, too, flat, beautifully flat, but also very colorful, like a peacock.

What I'm saying is my sense of balance hasn't changed since I lost my ear. I have only a bandage now and a lot of hats to cover my deficiency, if you prefer to call it that.

He received my ear, and he says it's nice, but can I maybe not do it again. He's concerned about infections and public opinion, but I tell him not to worry. I never consider what other people think, and I have enough hydrogen peroxide to sanitize a thousand missing ears.

I take my balance and imbalance and sit by my living room window, watching the neighbors as they walk by my apartment building on their way back from the grocery store. It is late October: the leaves are changing, and the sun is low in the sky, casting my neighbors in an orange haze. The people are lovely in their complexity, and I wonder about the way their soft skin winds itself around their bodies, enclosing organs, minds, a whole lifetime of experiences. It gives me shivers, and I think of him, the way he surveyed my body one night, my head down to my legs, and told me to be careful when I was driving. You have to take care of yourself, he said, you're too important. And in that moment I knew that I was—that I was a body, mind, and more.

I spread my hand across the windowsill. I stick my tongue out and examine my reflection in the window. These are superficial choices, I know: the hand I use to hold him or the tongue I use to kiss, to taste-test the food I so lovingly prepare for him. Which will he appreciate most when he opens his mailbox, home from work and tired? Which will reveal the ever-expanding part of me that glows for him?

I send him the tip of my tongue as a sign of eyes-closed kisses, the soft exploration of one mouth by another, and as a gesture of my selflessness. I can always get by with one hand, but I have no backup tongues. For him, I send my one and only.

I go to the mall with my best friend. We pass by the soft pretzel booth, even though I love them and all their glorious saltiness. We pass the cookies and the sandwiches, and my friend gives me a sidelong glance, strangely drawn to my tongue-less mouth but too polite to stare. Yet she can be polite for only so long. We've known each other since third grade, and she's not timid. She takes me to the pretzel booth, and I politely decline while she buys herself a pretzel, tears it apart, and shoves it in her mouth right in front of me.

"Where's your tongue?" she asks. "What did you do with it?"

"I mailed it," I say. "And just the tip." My words come out garbled, but I have nothing to be ashamed of.

"Of course you did. Did it ever occur to you that maybe you needed your tongue?"

I say nothing. Her questions are logical, and my answers are not. I'm not stupid. I knew I needed my tongue, but I also knew my tongue was a small gesture in a grand scheme. It was nothing really.

"This is what they do in some South American countries," she informs me, chewing with her mouth open. This is not her most ladylike moment. "They kidnap people who might have money, demand ransom, and then mail the families the victims' tongues and other body parts to prove they're serious." She continues to chew. There's a fleck of pretzel on her lip. "Is that what you're going for here?"

To my surprise, she has said it almost perfectly. "Yes," I attempt to say. "That's exactly what I'm doing, minus the ransom. I think of it as a gift."

"You couldn't just send flowers?" She shakes her head.

I know what she's getting at. There are so many people who self-destruct for the sake of another, but this feels different. I am not so much self-destructing as I am expanding, pushing my body as far as it will go until it can hold both him and me, a cocoon of air and organs and packing supplies.

"No," I say. "Flowers simply aren't good enough."

Afterward, I drive home slowly, angry drivers behind me, and I admire the sky, the clouds, the sun, the trees. It is all so very, very bright, and I am so lucky. And the more I give, the luckier I feel. I touch my hand to my forehead, consider my options.

An eye like a marble. An orb of bluish green. I send one and keep one. Although I know it's not possible, I hope that when he looks into my eye, he can see all that I see—the way the world has become impossibly sunny and I am forced to squint because whatever I do, I don't want to look away.

I try to send a kidney, but the post office won't let me. "It fits," I say, placing my neatly wrapped package in their one-size-fits-all box. It is soft and wet, and I have to move carefully for the sake of the kidney and my stitches, but I am determined.

"It's perishable," the woman at the counter says. "Among other things."

I want to explain that I've been sending perishable items all along, but it turns out that's part of the problem. My flat-rate boxes have been oozing unsightly liquids, emitting unseemly smells. "But that's natural," I say. "You know how nature works."

From the look she gives me, she does not know how nature works and doesn't especially want to know.

"The mail is delivered in the rain and the snow and sleet and hail," I plead. "Surely you can handle a little oozy box."

"No," she says. "We do not want to handle your oozy box."

There's no way around it, and I walk back outside, kidney held against my chest. The other customers in line gawk at me, some trying to see what I'm holding, some barely concealing their disdain at a repressive postal system that won't let a well-meaning patron mail her package when her item clearly fits. The whole world understands how I've been wronged.

Out on the step, I call him on my cell phone. I explain how I tried to mail a box, and it was going to be such a nice surprise for him, but the post office wouldn't let me.

"It's okay," he says. "You need your kidney anyway. How else are you going to filter out all those toxins?"

"What toxins?" I ask. "I don't have a toxic bone in my body." And it's true; I feel like everything ugly and mean has been filtered away, leaving a shimmering me.

He laughs at my answer, and that's enough. Somehow, some way, I'll get that kidney to him, but for now I have his voice in my ear, guiding me on my walk home. Once there, I separate the tips of my toes from my feet, little pellets of appreciation, wrap them in a napkin, and place them in my jacket pocket where I won't lose them. Another gift, I think. Another gift for another time.

The days are growing crisp with impending winter. I go for long walks, my jacket wrapped snugly around me. Soon it will be snowing; I can see it in the clouds, their gray downiness in the distance, slowly approaching, but I don't mind. Like everything else in my life, winter is burned gold around the edges by a light I can't see but can certainly feel.

I received a package in the mail the other day. A kidney carefully folded in Bubble Wrap and placed in Tupperware, not oozing. A kidney to replace my kidney. His kidney. I sensed solidarity in his gesture, solidarity against an unjust postal system and a generally hostile world. It felt good to have someone on my side, although I shouldn't have been surprised.

I am entering a new phase of my life, and he is in the middle and around the edges, and I'm not ashamed at all because I feel full and billowy. I could empty myself of everything—lungs, intestines, pancreas, heart—and there would always be more to give. I am like a starfish. I feel like I am capable of regenerating forever.

I pass by a party store and spot a collection of cherry-red balloons. My body is a collection of impulses, and I pass through the door, bells clanging, and buy all those balloons. I carry them down the street, helium hearts begging to be set free, and people turn to look. They smile despite the coming snow and the cold.

I take them to the park, my red entourage, and when I'm sure no one is looking, I spill the toes out of my pocket and tie one to the end of each balloon. I hold the balloons for a moment, admiring the way they stand out against the sky, wishing I could give more, wishing I could attach the piece of my brain that is responsible for all this swirling, golden joy—but that would require major surgery, and I simply can't afford it. I point the balloons in his general direction and set them free, watching as they tiptoe across the sky, a cloud of red ballooning as far as the eye can see, a scarlet wing that catches everything and holds it close.

Oh, Dr. Brown

He startles my body in ways I didn't know it could be startled. Drinks of water, vinegar, and cayenne pepper make my stomach turn, leave me light-headed and chilled. Before I leave he feeds me tiny chocolate bars laced with lavender and salt.

I am cleansing, or so he tells me. When this is all said and done I will be a better person, more in charge of my life than I have ever been before.

I can accept the fact that I am a person in need of cleansing. I go home at night and my apartment is falling apart around me. The dishes need to be washed, and some of them have been on the counter for a very long time. The floor needs to be swept. The edges of my bathtub are turning brown with soap: blue soap, yellow soap, all of those colored bars that have washed me clean, but have never been washed off the tub. There is a leak in my bedroom roof, and the floor below is always damp. I have buckets I could put beneath the leak, but I never think of them. Instead, I gaze in wonder when I come into my bedroom one day and see a small orange fungus rising from the carpet, reaching toward the sky, magnificent in its newfound life, born in a place it never imagined it would be.

The man who cleanses me asks me to refer to him as Doctor. Dr. Brown. I assume that Brown is not his real name, just as I assume that he is not really a doctor. His office is in the basement of his house. His house is in a shady part of the city, a neighborhood where the houses seem to slant to the side, exhausted with their place in this life, and many of them have boarded-up windows, victims of rocks and baseballs, kids who roam these streets with nothing better to do than to heave whatever happens to be in sight.

This is not a neighborhood I would ever drive through with my car doors unlocked. And yet I routinely come here, slip down into the basement of this man's falling-down house, and disrobe.

Sometimes I feel that my priorities are skewed.

More often I feel that I never really had any priorities to begin with. Everything I do has been dictated to me by an outside force: parents, friends, men I have dated who have tried to hijack my life, often with the best intentions. "Please lock your apartment door when you go to sleep at night," they said. "You never know who could try to get in."

I would awaken on those nights, hearing their voices in my head, knowing that my door was still unlocked, and I would hear sounds, all sorts of sounds coming from the living room. Many of the sounds were in my head, but some of them weren't. The apartment building was old with plenty of bending, creaking parts. And I would lay there listening, feeling more curious than afraid. If someone were to come in, who would it be? What would be this person's purpose in my apartment at this time of night?

I was never frightened.

Dr. Brown leads me down the steps into his office. It smells old and moldy, like damp newspapers and dirt, just the way a basement should. One wall is fully covered with shelves, which I imagine once held a family's pantry. Jars of jelly. Boxes of rice. Can upon can of soup and vegetables. Now the shelves house Dr. Brown's supplies: vinegar, pepper, apple juice, and many other bottles of liquids that are unmarked, unnamed. This is where most of the cleansing takes place.

In the center of the room is a massage table. Dr. Brown insists that cleansing a body begins with cleansing each muscle, ridding it of all the tension a muscle can harbor. He says that he trained to be a masseuse for many years. I had never had a massage before I met Dr. Brown. I have no way of knowing if his words or fingers are telling me the truth. All I know is that when I lie down on the table, I come close to losing myself in his touch, but I have never completely lost myself, just as I have never completely lost myself with anyone. I am simply there, hovering on the edge, feeling my muscles relax, watching the flickering of the candles out of the corner of my eye.

There are candles, too. There are always candles when Dr. Brown is involved.

He works in silence. I wish there could be music, but Dr. Brown says that music would interfere with the cleansing. He kneads my shoulders, the muscles along my back. He tells me I am very afraid. "That is the root of your troubles," he says. "All that fear."

I listen to him because he is my doctor. I drink the cleansing liquids he mixes for me in glasses painted with gaudy yellow flowers, the kind of glasses my grandma had before she modernized her kitchen and never turned back. I wait patiently as my body turns upon itself, roiling in shock as it digests the unmarked liquids it has been served.

When I am this sick, I feel apart from my body, a spirit on the ceiling watching myself convulse. I wonder if this is what it means to cleanse, to push your body so far to the edge that your soul goes running. I could ask Dr. Brown, but I don't have the strength to speak. My thoughts break into a million pieces. Words collapse.

Later, in the safety of my decrepit apartment, I consider this notion of fear. I have never thought of myself as afraid, but it might be so. There is plenty in the world to be afraid of: burglars, rapists, murderers, rare and deadly diseases, car accidents, leprechauns, death. And yet I have never really considered any of these things a threat.

I pour myself a glass of cranberry juice and vodka and think back.

I once stepped into oncoming traffic. There were so many cars, cars upon cars, and I was tired of waiting. Brakes squealed, horns blared, but I made it to the other side.

I once had a cat that had kittens. I remember watching her get larger and larger, her belly extending beyond her whiskers, throwing off her balance. Everyone who saw her was happy. Kittens, they told me. Soon your apartment is going to be filled with playing kittens. It's going to be so much fun.

I didn't see the fun, though. When I saw her waddling toward me, purring, eager to be petted, I felt only impending doom. My apartment wasn't a place for kittens. It wasn't even a place for me. I imagined them slipping into my soapy tub, breaking their tiny legs, and howling into the shower walls, shrieks of pain I wouldn't hear because I would be sleeping, or worse, not even home. I imagined them climbing the curtains, shredding the material with their claws, and then falling to the floor, unaware of how dangerous a shredded curtain could be. I couldn't follow these future kittens. I couldn't protect them from the world or even from themselves.

And so I gave my cat away before the kittens were even born. I was sad to see her go, but I felt weightless at the thought of a world without her.

And that was nothing compared with the pregnancy scare.

When I finish my cranberry vodka, I talk to the bird that replaced my cat. I tell him all about my day, my visit to Dr. Brown, the fact that the root of all my problems is that I'm afraid. The bird doesn't answer me. It's not even a talking bird. It's only a canary I bought at the pet store for fifteen dollars, a deal according to the salesman, despite the fact that there were many other canaries, each identical to my own.

I am waiting for Dr. Brown to mix me my cleansing drink when the police storm his basement. Before Dr. Brown even knows how to react, men in uniforms weighed down by pockets, so many pockets filled with radios and handcuffs and who knows what else, pin him to the wall and read him his rights. I watch the whole scene in silence. I'm not frightened.

After Dr. Brown is led away, one of the officers approaches me, asks if I'm all right. "All right?" I say. "Of course I'm all right. That was my doctor."

"He's not really a doctor." The officer looks me over. "We should take you to the hospital."

I ignore his suggestion. "If he's not a doctor, then what is he?"

"He's a scam artist."

I wonder what part of my treatment was a scam. Dr. Brown may not have been a doctor, but he made me feel better, sometimes. And he tried to understand me. Wasn't that the first part of healing? Understanding?

The officer takes my arm. "Really," he says. "We should get you to the hospital."

I shake him off. I don't want to go to the hospital. "I don't feel sick," I say. "We weren't even to the cleansing yet."

He doesn't know what I'm talking about, but he doesn't have to. I'm not going to the hospital, and my fierce expression tells him so. I cross my arms over my chest and stare him down until he says fine and backs away up the stairs.

I am finally alone in the basement. I survey the massage table, the candles that have been blown out and are cooling, the light that tumbles through the tiny windows above. In this moment, the office has lost its magic. It's just a basement once again, a dream rejected by reality.

I turn to the shelves stacked with marked and unmarked liquids. Without thinking about what I'm doing, I take an unmarked jar, stuff it under my shirt, and hurry up the stairs to where the police are waiting to take down my name, number, and statement. All the petty details of my existence. All the details that aren't even worth remembering.

I don't get in my car.

I wait for the police to drive away, and then I begin to walk. The October sun shines down on me, bright, tenuous. The leaves burn red and yellow and brown. I shuffle under them, through them. I wish I could shield my eyes.

There is always too much. Too much to see. Too much to feel.

I think of the baby. The baby I thought I was going to have. I remember sitting down on the couch once I realized I was late. I remember the ache in my chest, my abdomen, the way the room swirled. I remember thinking: feet, kicking feet; hands, tiny hands; and a mind, a mind like mine.

That was what scared me the most—that mind.

I come to a coffee shop tucked into the bottom of an old brick building, and without making a conscious decision to do so, I step inside and order a latte. I take a seat by the window and watch the people stroll past. A few tables over, a man catches my eye, stares at me like I am a cherry Danish.

I am not afraid of him. I am composed of nothing he can take.

I remember the day I understood my mind. I was four years old and my mom was driving me home from day care. The car windows were rolled down to let in the sunlight, the fresh summer air, and I thought: *I exist. I exist and I am separate.* And in the glory of that existence, that separation, came the knowledge of a whole vast world bearing down on me, a world that was never going to go away. It was amazing then. It became less amazing with time.

The man a few tables over continues to watch me. When it seems like I might notice him, he smiles. He might be the one to save me, assuming I can be saved. I don't really assume anything. I reach under my coat, pull out the unmarked bottle. I pour the liquid into my coffee, more liquid than Dr. Brown ever prescribed for me, set the cup aside, and gaze out the window at the pressing shades of the passing day, wondering how much I must break myself in order to feel better.

The Invisible Boy

It is hard to be an invisible boy, traipsing along the backyard while mom is inside taking a nap with "Uncle Rob." Uncle Rob is not really an uncle and Rob is not really his name. His real name is Brian, but he prefers to be Rob because as he puts it, "Rob is short and tough. A man's name."

The boy likes to think he has a man's name: Chet, although the *ch* sound is soft and the way his mom says it, tucking him in at night, saying "Good night, Chet," makes him feel like a little kid, but he is eight years old and well on his way to manhood, or so his dad says when he's actually around.

But now Chet is not Chet, but is rather the invisible boy, swinging on his aluminum swing set like a ghost, jumping from the highest point and landing on both his feet, his body absorbing the impact in a rush that moves from feet to knees to chest. He is a superhero, and if he could find an even higher point to jump from, the top of the house maybe or the old oak tree, he would, but there is no way up to those places, no way that he can think of, and so he draws pictures on the rainy days. Pictures of him jumping from the roof, green cape aloft because Superman has already claimed the red one and, besides, he has to blend in with the forest, which is his true home. Pictures of him flying through the air like a kind of bird, like a kind of plane, not unlike Superman.

But these are only thoughts inside his head, which is always, always hard at work, and the rest is silence punctuated by the occasional screech of the swings and the birds and the wind moving past his ears. Then he is bored with the swing and continues his ghostly trek to the edge of the woods, which is as far as he can go. The rest is forbidden. "Forbidden," his dad told him once, emphasizing the sound, and so now he always stops at this point and peers as far into the brush and trees as he possibly can, imagining the exciting things he might see within.

Then he is moving back, taking the long way around the perimeter of the yard past the newly constructed shed, placed there by Uncle Rob so that he would have room to store his motorcycle, which is shiny and broad and fills the boy with a deep loathing every time he looks at it. He passes this shed quickly because it is a stranger to this lawn, but not quickly enough because he is suddenly stopped by a nail piercing through his foot, entering the soft, soft skin between two fragile bones and continuing up, up, and invisibility fades as his screams fill the air, and he hops, then falls, watching the blood pour, not in a trickle but in a long stream that covers weeds and grass and the dirt below, and he is crying, crying and his mom is there, pulling on his foot, shaking her head, and lifting him, eight years old, to the car, where she hurries him off to the emergency room.

At the hospital, everything is routine. The fluorescent lights shine down until they create a buzzing in his head that will later be a headache his mom tries to heal with water. "You cried so much," she'll say. "You're probably dehydrated." The smells seep in and remind him of a bathroom after a good cleaning, only worse, and he feels dizzy as the doctor takes X-rays, then slowly removes the nail from his foot while he looks away, holding his mom's hand even though he is close to being a man now. Then there is a shot deep within his arm that aches even though he refuses to say so, and his mom is called out to complete paperwork because apparently there is a lot of information to give when a person comes to the hospital and has to have a nail removed from his foot.

What isn't routine is the doctor returning to the room and closing the door softly behind him. He takes a seat in front of the boy and says, "I'm not supposed to do this, but I thought you might like this as a reminder of your war wound." And he holds up the nail, still encrusted with the boy's blood, and the boy stares at it a moment, this object that caused him so much pain, before he cups it in his own hand and thanks the doctor.

"You're welcome," the doctor says. "Next time be careful where you step." And he tousles the boy's hair, which is annoying but not completely unwelcome. Then he is gone, leaving the boy alone again.

For an afternoon, the boy is less invisible. His mom lets him sit on the couch—she usually sends him outside on sunny days so that he won't become "one of those couch potatoes"—and she props his foot up on the footstool and tells him to pick out a movie. "*Dracula*," he says, pointing to the DVD he has been eyeing for months, and his mom shakes her head because that movie is forbidden, but then she looks at him and relents. It's been a long day for both of them and perhaps he is old enough now. Perhaps he won't find it too scary, and if he does, if he spends half the night awake from nightmares, he shouldn't come crying to her.

The movie is all he thought it would be and more. There are vampires and dead girls and wolves and even vampires who turn themselves into mist so they can slip under doors and float through the night sky like clouds, and in his mind he adds that to his repertoire of superhero abilities. There is flying, and then there is becoming a mist. There is becoming a wolf, but maybe he'd rather become a deer. They're graceful.

He continues to debate these points during dinner when Uncle Rob asks him how his foot is and then turns to his mom and begins questioning her about what she's going to plant in the garden and what he should do about a situation at work, and his mom is all ears and the boy becomes invisible again. He could become a deer, but then he would be at the mercy of wolves and dogs, although he doesn't think there are many wolves around here. He could become a fox, and that might be a better choice because they are sleek and agile and smart, but an owl might also be a good choice if he's going to be a creature of the night.

His mind is still racing when his mom tucks him into bed, accentuating the softness of his name—"Good night, Chet"—and reminding him to wake her up if he wants another Tylenol. He only half listens because he realizes he doesn't have to limit himself to just one animal, but rather can become a shape-shifter, which is exciting indeed, and he turns to face the window, imagining all the creatures he could be.

A few hours later he wakes up to a throbbing foot. It feels hot and swollen under the sheets, and he considers getting his mom, but that would mean encountering Uncle Rob, who stays over almost every night now. So he forces the pain from his mind and turns to the window and the cool night air and wonders if there are any vampires out there. If so, could his interest inadvertently

The Sadness of Spirits

invite them in? Could his thoughts accidentally bring a vampire to his home?

He feels nervous thinking about that and so he instead turns to the nail, which he hid in the top drawer of his bedside table. He turns it over in his hand, remembering the feel of it piercing through his foot, and the blood. He has never felt that much pain before, at least not physically, and he considers the power of this nail. If birds eat spiders to gain their power and people eat birds to gain their power and vampires eat people to gain their power, then maybe he can put this nail to good use. And he does, popping it in his mouth and turning it over on his tongue, tasting cool metal, the copper of his own blood, before swallowing it down in one, two painful gulps.

The boy cannot eat breakfast. It hurts to swallow his oatmeal and it hurts to sit and it hurts to stand and walk from the table to the couch, where his mom instructs him to go when she presses a hand to his forehead and realizes he is running a fever. On the couch, he drifts into the background as his mom makes call after call, first to his grandma to see if she has any advice, then to the doctor, then to her boss, then to Uncle Rob to let him know what's going on. She talks to Uncle Rob for a long time and ends the call with "I love you," which brings back memories of his dad in a way that is like having his stomach twisted around, but in a worse way than it already is.

What follows is routine: they return to the hospital and there are more X-rays, more blood tests. Then he is wheeled into a room where everything is both too bright and too dark, and a nurse puts a mask over his face and instructs him to count backward from one hundred. When he wakes up there is a long line of stitches across his stomach and the nail he carried around inside him is gone and his stomach hurts more than it ever has in his whole life. The room spins and he is nauseous and his mom is there, bending over him, angry. "What were you thinking?" she asks. "Why would you ever eat a nail? How did you even get it?"

Somehow he knows better than to blame the doctor.

There are hospital expenses, she continues, expenses they can't afford, and he is *eight years old*; he should know better than to go sticking things in his mouth where they don't belong.

There is nothing to say in the face of her wrath, although his own anger is building because he knows why he did it. She would never understand because she doesn't know the things he knows: about superheroes, about strength, about finding power in whatever small places you can, and so he silently fumes until she finally says that she has to go to work, she couldn't take the whole day off for him, and then she is gone, leaving him alone in this hospital room that feels a little too white, a little too quiet, and a little too big for one boy alone.

There is time for his stomach to heal: days spent in the cool quiet of his bedroom, surrounded by books and action figures, days spent on the couch watching movies. His grandparents come to visit, and they bring him a toy fire truck to drive across the couch cushions, and he likes it, although it reminds him of his dad, which brings back that familiar ache in his stomach. His dad pulling on the fire gear he kept at the house for emergencies, when he would drive directly to the scene. His dad coming home smelling of smoke and sweat. The boy leans against his grandpa, who has a tanned and leathery face, kind and often smiling, and who is somewhat like his dad, and listens to him tell his stories, but it's just not the same. His dad never once comes to visit.

He grows bored, which his mom says is a good thing because he's healing, but it doesn't feel like a good thing to him because the days stretch before him, long and uninterrupted. His mom says he is old enough to stay home by himself—eight years old means he's a big boy—but there is a list of things he is forbidden to do: no going outside, no climbing up the stairs, no jumping of any kind. His stitches are fragile, she says. They can't afford another doctor's visit.

And so he sits alone on the couch, watching TV. Most days he's by himself, but sometimes Uncle Rob is there with him, sleeping in his mom's bedroom until close to eleven. "Be quiet for Uncle Rob," his mom tells him before she leaves, and he wants to ask her why when Uncle Rob is never considerate of him, but he doesn't ask this because she would, as she herself puts it, smack him upside the head, and so he is quiet and he watches TV quietly and he pours cereal quietly and he thinks quiet thoughts about how much he hates Uncle Rob and how if he could only grow wings he would leave this house and show them all just how special he really is.

On this particular morning, he watches TV until his feet twitch and his legs twitch and his whole body is twitching with energy. He can't sit still, but he also can't go outside, and so he stands and walks to his mom's bedroom door. He leans close and listens to Uncle Rob's snores, and he feels a boiling in his chest that has been going on since Uncle Rob began showing up on the afternoons when his dad was at work. For a while it seemed that Uncle Rob was showing up more and more and his dad less and less until his dad wasn't around at all, replaced by this blond man with his fake smile and his motorcycle.

The boy pushes the door open slowly. He isn't supposed to bother Uncle Rob, but Uncle Rob bothers him. The air is musty and heavy even though the air conditioner is going full blast, and he can just make out the hulking shape of Uncle Rob beneath the blankets. Even though the whir of the air conditioner covers the sound of his footsteps, he tiptoes across the room and stops before the bed. Uncle Rob is breathing heavily and the boy can smell his morning breath, his sweat. His arms are thrust across the bed like a doll, and for the first time it dawns on the boy how fragile a man really is.

The boy hovers and then steps away. He makes his way to the dresser, where he opens first one drawer and then another, searching, searching until he comes across a little cardboard box. Taking the box in his hands and casting another glance at Uncle Rob, he slips from the room and closes the door behind him.

The living room isn't safe, and so the boy shuts himself in the bathroom. Flipping on the fluorescent light, he sets the box on the counter, opens it up, and begins taking its contents out one by one: a man's ring, a watch, extra buttons for flannel shirts, a package of cigarettes, a lighter, a Swiss Army knife—all the little objects his dad left behind and his mom hid away. He runs his fingers across the watch, lifts a cigarette from the package and sniffs it, and then takes out two buttons. They are smooth and clear and plastic, no larger than a dime, and they bring back memories of being held close to his father's chest.

He takes each button and places it on his tongue. They are easy to swallow and don't get caught in his throat. The Swiss Army knife goes in his pocket, and he hides the box under the sink behind a stack of old towels to be revisited another time.

He spends the rest of the day contented, two buttons resting on his stomach floor.

The boy is back outside in no time, although swinging and jumping are still forbidden. Summer is in full force, and since he can't entertain himself through movement he takes to the dirt, gathering grasshoppers into jars and wiping their spit off his hands and rooting through the grass for worms and ants to pick up and examine. "You're getting yourself dirty," his mom says, but he doesn't care. There's a whole world down there he's never stopped to investigate before.

The buttons ride along safely. They don't cause him any trouble.

He is holding a woolly bear caterpillar, soft streaks of black and brown curled in his palm, when Uncle Rob calls to him. "Hey," he says. "Come help me with this wood."

Slowly, the boy draws himself up and trots to the driveway, where Uncle Rob is opening the bed of his pickup truck to reveal a great pile of freshly chopped wood. "It's about time you started helping out around the place," Uncle Rob says. "Start stacking over there." And he points to the side of the shed where the rest of the wood is piled beneath a blue tarp.

The boy stands next to the truck and waits to receive the wood. He is silent on the outside, as always, but inside is a seething array of anger and injustice. He always did chores around the house before Uncle Rob arrived, helping his dad to stack wood and plant seeds in the garden and rake grass clippings. Uncle Rob just never asked, and he can't be expected to read minds.

He thinks of the buttons within him, though, and decides to copy some of his dad's patience. "You have to be smarter than other people," his dad told him once when other kids were picking on him at school. "You have to be patient and outthink them."

It won't be hard to outthink Uncle Rob. He doesn't seem especially bright.

He clutches each log carefully to his chest, mindful of his stitches, those fine bits of thread holding skin to skin, but even when he moves carefully he can feel them pulling against each other, and after many trips from the truck to the woodpile and back again his whole body feels like it is pulling apart, arms from shoulder blades, neck from back, and he would stop to rest except that Uncle Rob is urging him to go faster. "We don't have all day," he says. "I have to work tonight."

"My stitches," the boy says.

"Your stitches are just about healed," replies Uncle Rob. "Let me give you some life advice. Don't complain when you're hurt. You don't want to show other people weakness."

The boy feels like he should be grateful to Uncle Rob for sharing advice with him in the way that his father would or his grandfather would, but there is no kindness in Uncle Rob's voice, and before the boy can reply, Uncle Rob has already turned back to the wood and is rapidly lowering yet another log into the boy's aching arms and he is pulling himself together under the weight and his abdomen is beginning to feel misplaced, as if part of his skin has slid into a place it's not supposed to be, and to distract himself he thinks of the caterpillar huddled in the grass, prophesizing the winter, and the grasshoppers hopping far and free. He wonders what that feeling is like, to not be under the control of the moms and Uncle Robs of the world.

Then they are done and this is one thing the boy is just beginning to learn: some bad things come to an end—the ache of surgery, a dreaded afternoon of carrying wood—while some bad things do not—his desire to be grown up, for instance, and the way he misses his dad. Uncle Rob closes the truck bed, and without saying a word to him—no thank you, no good job—he goes into the house presumably to take a shower and nap before work, leaving the boy to his own devices once again. The boy takes one step toward the backyard, but in the sudden exhaustion of carrying the wood, he sits down in the grass beside the woodpile, closes his eyes, and listens to the bird calls, the sound of the wind rustling the trees. Without meaning to, he is remembering Uncle Rob in bed, the sheet drawn over his body, the soft breath coming out of the O of his mouth. He could take a pillow in his hand, push it down over his mouth, and then lean on it with all of his weight. He could light a match and lock the door.

The Sadness of Spirits

None of this is realistic, though. Just fantasies he would never act on. Instead, he opens his eyes and studies the woodpile towering over him. So much wood from so many trees, all of them solid and tall and stately. He raises a hand and lets his fingers meander over the bark. Even though the trees are dead, they will still retain their shape, their being for many seasons before eventually giving way to burrowing ants and other bugs. He carefully pulls a strip of bark from a log, examining it in his hand, this small piece of something so much larger than himself, before placing it in his mouth and chewing. It goes from hard to gummy, and he swallows it with some difficulty and then stands up. He has to think small if he's going to get back at Uncle Rob. He has to outsmart him.

There are plenty of gravel rocks in the driveway, and he is careful to select one with a sharp point. He moves to the front end of the truck, selecting a place slightly over the driver's side wheel well, and presses the rock deep into the paint. He hesitates for a moment, using his laser vision to try to imagine all the consequences and repercussions, but all he can really think of is how this will affect Uncle Rob. The moment he goes to open the door and sees the scratch in the paint. The hopeless feeling of knowing his truck is forever ruined.

The boy grips the rock, willing himself to move, but then he can't. Uncle Rob will know that it was him, and he'll get in trouble. Besides, he knows better than to damage other people's things.

He tosses the rock back into the driveway and heads inside. There will be other ways. He just has to keep thinking.

The boy is invisible during dinner, which doesn't surprise him. Uncle Rob is focused on his plate, trying to eat fast before he goes to work, and his mom carries on a conversation mostly with herself. "I saw Tina at the grocery store," she says. "Did you know that she's expecting another baby?"

"Is that so?" says Uncle Rob, and continues to shovel food. "That will make three. A full house."

The boy wonders if his mom is planning another baby and if he will have to share his room, but he doesn't think about it long because she is talking about Grandma and Grandpa and how they will be coming over for dinner on Sunday and does Uncle Rob want to have ham or roast beef? Chocolate cake or lemon meringue pie?

The boy's attention wanders. His stomach is churning, and he wonders if it's the bark. Maybe the tree was poisonous and the poison is slowly seeping from his stomach to all his other organs. He imagines himself growing tired and collapsing, maybe when he's doing the dishes or maybe when he's brushing his teeth for bed. Either way his mom will come running and lift him up as she did the day he stepped on the nail. She'll drive him straight to the hospital and sit weeping in the waiting room while she waits for the doctor's verdict. And Uncle Rob will be there, too, sorry for the way he treated the boy just that afternoon.

"Chet," his mom is saying. "Chet, we're talking to you."

He looks up and it seems that only his mom is talking to him since Uncle Rob is still focused on his plate. "Sorry," he says. "I didn't hear you."

"I was saying that someone has a birthday coming up." She smiles at him. "Any idea what you want?"

He knows exactly what he wants, but he can't come up with the right words. Instead, he thinks up a more acceptable answer. "An insect collecting kit," he says. "And a tent."

"An insect collecting kit?" she repeats. "What is that?"

"I saw it in a magazine. It has a net and a jar to keep insects in and a magnifying glass."

"Do you really need to buy a kit for that?" Uncle Rob asks, looking up. "I'm sure you can put that together from junk around the house."

"We'll think about it," his mom says, but the boy can hardly pay attention. He is imagining foraging the yard with his dad, putting grasshoppers in a jar.

"Now, why do you need a tent?" his mom continues. "You know the woods are off-limits."

He forces his mind back to the present, to his mom's inquisitive look, Uncle Rob's steely gaze. He's pretty sure he's never done anything seriously wrong, but Uncle Rob still looks at him like he's about to burn the house down, or worse, whatever that might be. "I know the woods are off-limits," he says. "I just thought that maybe I could sleep in the backyard when it's warm out."

His mom turns to Uncle Rob and he shrugs. "I don't see any harm in it. If he wants to sleep on the ground, then let him sleep on the ground."

"We'll see," his mom says. "No promises." Which is how it is every birthday and Christmas. The boy doesn't get his hopes up for anything.

He hesitates now and there it is, the question he really wants to know the answer to slowly bubbling to the surface. Before he can hold back it is out, breathlessly, hanging on the air between them. "Will Dad be coming?"

His mom looks at him carefully. "No," she says, finally. "I don't think he'll be coming."

"Why not?" He knows he shouldn't push, but he does anyway.

Her mouth opens and then closes, but she doesn't answer. "Tell him the truth," Uncle Rob says. "He's old enough to know. Your dad left the state. He won't be driving back just for your birthday."

The boy's head buzzes with this new information. He left the state? Where did he go? Why didn't he say where he was going? "Do you know where he is?"

Uncle Rob looks at the boy's mom. "Tennessee. He moved there with his girlfriend."

He has a girlfriend, too. And from there the boy's imagination fills with possibilities. A girlfriend can mean other kids: other boys, other girls, a completely different family, and he has been left behind.

"It doesn't mean your dad doesn't care," his mom is saying, but he hardly hears her. His dad could have taken him. He is sure of this. He could have swooped in and taken him along because there is nothing his dad can't do, but he chose not to. He chose to leave him alone with his mom and Uncle Rob.

"Things just change. And he has to make his own life."

The boy was supposed to be his life. And his mom. But Uncle Rob had to come over on the afternoons and his mom had to let him in and now their lives have been ruined and his dad is gone and won't even come over for his birthday. It's their fault, he thinks. It's their fault his dad is gone, and his stomach churns at the thought of this and he wants to get up and run, leave this silent dinner table and the creaking house far behind, but the rules dictate that leaving the table before everyone is done eating is forbidden, and so he draws all these feelings in until he is sinking, sinking into himself, and his mom has resumed her cheery voice, which he really hates sometimes. "You can still have a nice birthday dinner," she's saying. "What would you like?"

"Spaghetti," he says, not because he cares but because it's something to say.

"Spaghetti, please," corrects Uncle Rob.

"Spaghetti, please."

"And a chocolate cake?"

"A chocolate cake, please."

He has gone from himself to a wind-up version of a boy, and he wishes the bark poison would finally take effect, but there is no rescue until Uncle Rob takes the last slow bite and he is finally free to wash the dishes and take out the garbage and disappear to his room, where he takes the Swiss Army knife out of his pocket and flicks it open and closed. He imagines his dad watching TV on the couch, his new girlfriend and children gathered at his side, and wonders how he could be replaced. Doesn't his dad miss him? Doesn't he want to visit for his birthday?

Outside, Uncle Rob's truck starts up and pulls out of the driveway, gravel crunching beneath the tires. The boy should have scratched the truck when he had the chance. He should have kicked it hard with his shoes.

There's a knock at his door, and then his mom is stepping inside without waiting for him to answer. "What are you doing?" she asks.

"Nothing. Just looking out the window." He slips the pocket-knife beneath the covers.

She sits down on the edge of the bed. "I know you're upset about your dad not coming for your birthday."

He says nothing. The night air is warm, and he wishes he were out there, free beneath the stars. With or without a tent, it doesn't matter.

"And I know you probably think it's my fault," she continues. "Me and Uncle Rob both."

He remains silent. It is their fault, but he knows better than to say that.

"I just want you to know that things are complicated." She carefully stretches the bedspread with her hand, not making eye contact. "There's more to the situation than you understand. Things weren't always good between me and your dad."

He wants to tell her that it wasn't just about her, that he was part of the family, too, but he only nods, and she takes this as a sign of forgiveness. "You'll understand when you're older." She bends to kiss his forehead and tousle his hair, which used to be nice but now only makes him burn inside, the bark and buttons churning in a fury. "For now, let's just concentrate on you having a nice birthday."

She turns out the light as she leaves, leaving him alone to think about how little his birthday matters. His presence doesn't seem to matter. Even if he was poisoned from the bark and went to the hospital and died, everyone would mourn for a while and move on and he would be forgotten. The world and the order of events that presented themselves were not as they seemed and not what he expected them to be. Things were either safe or they were forbidden. Families raised children and children grew up and started families of their own. Uncles didn't interfere. Fathers didn't leave.

If everyone else has the right to break the rules, he thinks, then he doesn't have to follow them either. He sinks far below his sheets, listening to the night, listening to the creaking of floorboards as his mom moves from the living room to the bathroom to the bedroom, listening for that shift of air that signals she's asleep. He turns the pocketknife over in his hand as he waits, planning out the way he will quickly move to the closet for his jacket and stop at the front door for his shoes before flicking the lock, turning the knob quietly, and running off into the night.

The boy is circling in the woods, moving in directions he doesn't understand. First meandering to the left. Then meandering to the right. His backyard—that safe world of cut grass and swing sets and a single willow tree he loves to climb—isn't that far away, a few hundred yards at most, but the night is a tumble of darkness and twigs and stars too distant to guide his way, and besides, home is the one direction he doesn't want to go. He stumbles over raised roots and pushes his way through shrubs and brambles and bushes. His bare arms and legs are scratched and his stomach aches with the effort of moving, but he is pure forward momentum. The forest is forbidden, and he is in it. The buttons and bark give him strength and dimension, and he moves as fast as he can until the eastern sky begins to glow golden, and he falls beneath a tree and drifts off to sleep.

He wakes up and it takes a moment to remember where he is. Nothing is familiar: not the brush where he is hidden, not the trees spreading their dark canopy above, not the weak, queasy feeling in his stomach. Fear overtakes him in dark, cold sweats, and he pulls the Swiss Army knife from his pocket and flicks it open and closed, watching the way the morning sunlight hits the blade. Then he stands. There is nothing to do but walk.

He could walk back to the house, and that is what he does at first, attempting to retrace his steps, but as he walks he remembers his mom and Uncle Rob and his dad living in another state with another family, and he stops. If he can stay hidden long enough, he reasons, they will have to contact his dad and his dad will have to come and find him. He'll be angry and accuse his mom of not being a good mother, and then the boy will get to go live with him.

He sees it all clearly in his head, and without giving it any further thought, he turns around and pushes his way deeper into the woods. The Allegheny Forest is huge, he knows. A person can get lost there for days, especially if he wants to get lost.

The sun is high in the sky, almost noon. The boy knows this just as he knows some other facts his dad taught him about the great outdoors. He recites them one by one, taking comfort in his knowledge:

1. All caterpillars are safe to touch, except for the white spiked ones. Brown woolly caterpillars can predict the future.
2. Caterpillars become butterflies and lose their future-predicting properties.
3. Trees grow from seeds.
4. Birds carry seeds for many miles, which is how family trees become so spread.
5. He carries seeds for many miles when they attach themselves to his clothes, to his hair.

6. Moss only grows on the north side of the tree.
7. If you talk to trees, then trees will think back to you in a silent way that can be interpreted only as telepathy.

He takes pride in knowing these facts and recites them to himself again and again, sometimes adding in the longer explanations his dad once gave him. He pretends he is speaking to a great crowd of people interested in his wilderness skills. He has lived in the forest for many years, wears a coonskin hat, and has a lot to share. When he is done speaking, they applaud and his mom's eyes fill with tears. Uncle Rob is not allowed to attend.

These thoughts keep his mind from his stomach, which has transitioned from queasy to growling. If he had been thinking, he would have taken some food the night before, bread or crackers or something, but it's not a big deal. This is only one more test of his skills. He has his knife and so eventually he can make a bow and arrow or a fishing rod. He'll need some string, of course, but you never know what you'll find out in the woods, what campers will leave behind, although he hasn't seen signs of other people quite yet.

In the meantime, he stops by a tree with a great white trunk and bark that is already peeling off. He takes a strip and puts it in his mouth. It is ugly and bitter, much worse than the bark of the day before, but he forces himself to chew it down to a gum and swallow. Then he does it again and again. His stomach fights with every downed bite, but he tells himself that this is what being a wilderness man is all about, rising to challenges and overcoming them.

His dad could be a wilderness man. He rescues people and pets from burning buildings, rushing into the flames and carrying them out doors and windows and sometimes places where walls used to be. He would come home smelling of smoke and soot and still have the energy for a hug.

He imagines his dad would be very proud of him right now.

He circles and traipses and tries to be as quiet as possible until he finds something that seems helpful to him: a small, trickling creek. A creek, his dad told him on one of their walks, is important. If you follow water, you won't get lost.

And if you have water, then you won't get thirsty. He bends to the ground and tries to slurp up as much as he can, but the water only makes his stomach gurgle more and he backs away. Instead, he opts for a smooth, round pebble that he places on his tongue and sucks on, imagining that he's draining as much water as possible from it. Pebble tucked in his mouth, he begins to follow the creek, taking step after limping step, putting as much distance as possible between himself and the house.

They will eventually find him; this he knows. His dad told him that the search and rescue dogs never fail. Once scented, they always find their prey. The boy imagines police and firefighters and dogs spreading through the woods like a great balloon that will overtake him. He'll be fishing at the creek and there they'll be, expecting to find him on the verge of death, but he'll calmly welcome them, invite them into the cottage he's constructed of sticks and brush and leaves. His dad will be on the search and rescue team and the boy will be overjoyed to see him, but he'll be careful not to get too emotional in front of all those people.

His stomach aches again, a swelling on the inside that is indistinguishable from the pain on the outside. He places his hand against his stitches, and it comes away damp and sticky. He needs some sort of medicine, but that's one part of his plan he hasn't thought through. Perhaps he could wash his stitches at the creek, but that sounds painful and he simply continues on.

It is almost sunset when he stops beside the creek, suddenly aware of the mistake he's made. All day he has been following the water, stopping occasionally to pick up a new pebble and suck all the moisture out of it before swallowing it down, but now he realizes that if he can follow the water, then anyone else can, too. He thinks back to his dad holstering a gun to his hip before their forest walks, how he asked, "Is that for bears?"

"Maybe, but there are more dangerous things in the woods."

"Like what?"

"People. You never know who you're going to find."

The situation becomes clear to him: not only does the creek make it easier for his mom and Uncle Rob to find him, but it also means he might run into a stranger, a dangerous stranger who has escaped into the woods. The boy hesitates on the edge of the water, weighing the likelihood of meeting someone at this time of day against the shadowy trees beyond, then he fills his pockets with three more stones and hurries as far away from the water as he can possibly get.

His stomach is a strange configuration of hunger and pain and nausea. Shooting pains roll all the way down his abdomen, and it's hard to say what is on the inside and what is on the outside, what is caused by hunger and what isn't. The night presses in, cold and dark, and he finds himself yearning for dinner and for his bed, but instead he huddles beneath a tree, his shorts and shirt nowhere near thick enough to protect him from the dew.

He feels safe for now, but only because he believes nothing will be able to see him in the darkness. He's such a small boy, and no one has ever noticed him before.

He distracts himself with escapes. The scenario is the following: he is walking through the woods and there, directly in front of him, is a frenzied man with a hatchet. The man isn't obviously frenzied since he believes himself to be alone in the forest, but the boy knows his madness is hidden just below the surface. The boy will see the man before the man sees him. This is simply a fact since the boy is small and quiet and lower to the ground. The boy will then

The Sadness of Spirits

proceed to lower himself farther into the brush, again soundlessly, while also backing away. Then, when he has reached a reasonable distance, he will run as fast as he can, and the man with the hatchet will never catch him.

If the man gets close, the boy can make a swift turn and throw him off his tracks.

The boy can throw rocks at him.

The boy can climb a tree.

He shivers and the cold comes from deep within him, even though his face feels warm, hot even. He lifts one pebble out of his pocket, runs his finger across its smooth surface, and then puts it back again. His dad is out there somewhere, perhaps even in these woods, clearing a path, calling the boy's name. Maybe the boy won't have a cottage ready and won't be able to offer his rescuers any fish, but he'll still be happy to see his dad and he'll have quite the story to tell when school starts in the fall. "I lived in the forest for many days," he'll tell his astounded schoolmates, "and I ate only rocks."

Of course, Uncle Rob will be gone by then. His mom will have seen the error of her ways.

He draws his knees up to his chest, but even this isn't enough to stop his shaking. He closes his eyes and listens to the night birds. Sleep doesn't come.

The following morning, his limbs ache so much he has trouble standing. He takes one wobbly step and then another, steadying himself against trees. His head spins and his abdomen is a criss-crossed map of shooting pains that take his breath away. Water would be perfect, but he is far, far away from the creek and has no idea how to get back. He walks a ways and then rests, walks farther and then rests again. He wishes the search and rescue team would hurry up and find him.

The man sees him long before he sees the man. Gaunt and gray-haired with a flannel shirt, worn-out jeans, and a straw hat, the man stands in a slight clearing and asks, "What are you doing out here? This isn't a place for kids to be alone."

The boy freezes. He needs to sink down, run away, throw stones, but his head is hot pain and he can think only about the raspy edge of the man's voice, how it feels like it could cut right through him.

"What's wrong with you, boy?" the man asks. "Can't you talk?"

He wobbles on his legs, turns to go, but black spots are floating before his eyes. He's never seen anything like them before, and as much as he blinks they won't go away. Instead, they gather faster and faster until everything is going black and the man's hand is on his arm, steadying him before he falls.

There are two dogs. One, with a head like soft velvet, wakes the boy, nudging him gently with its nose and staring at him with yearning brown eyes. The other dog sits in the corner and watches the boy warily. When the boy moves too much, the dog lowers its head and growls.

This catches the man's attention, and he comes over to the makeshift bed where the boy is lying. "You're awake," he says. "How are you feeling?"

The boy looks around slowly. He's in a house, but it's not much of a house. The floors are dirt and the walls are made out of wood with bits of bright Pink Panther insulation showing through here and there. A single fireplace stands at the end of the room along with an old wooden table. He's on some sort of hard cot, but it feels good to rest his body.

"I'm okay," he says. "Feeling better."

The man nods. "You're not out of the woods yet."

The boy stares at him, trying to understand what this means. The man reminds him of his grandpa because of his gray beard and the tobacco smell that follows him everywhere, but he is not the boy's grandpa. His eyes are serious and distant. He doesn't smile when he talks.

"I don't know what you did to yourself," he continues, "but your stitches are infected. I tried to clean it out, but I don't have much here. Some aspirin and soap is about all. Where did you come from?"

"My house," he begins, but then he stops. His head is still spinning, and he's suddenly not sure if he should reveal where his mom lives. "I don't remember."

"You don't remember where you live?" The man stands up and walks over to the fireplace. "That's not exactly helpful."

The boy is silent. The velvet-haired dog has moved to the far side of the room, and he wishes it would come back.

"What about your parents?" the man asks. "What are their names?"

The boy hesitates. "I don't know."

The man turns around. "What do you mean you don't know your parents' names? Don't lie to me."

The boy says nothing. His parents' names aren't his to share.

"You're only making it harder for yourself." The man stirs something in a pot over the fire. "My brother will be coming tomorrow, and he'll take you into town."

Into town. The boy tries to imagine what this will consist of: life in the brother's basement, slavery, torture, and death. He tries to sit up, but his head is still fuzzy, and those black dots return to the edge of his vision. "Can I call my parents?" he asks.

"So you remember your phone number." The man shakes his head. "No, you can't call your parents. I don't have a phone."

The boy sinks back down onto the cot. What kind of person doesn't have a phone? What kind of person lives out in the woods with just two dogs? He makes eyes contact with the velvet-haired dog across the room and tries to will it back, but the dog remains seated.

"Here," the man says, slopping some thick white liquid from the pot into a bowl. "Eat this."

He places the bowl in front of the boy, along with a spoon, and the boy again forces himself to sit up. The soup is like nothing he's ever seen before—thick and white with floating potatoes and something dark and rubbery. There could be danger in the soup, poison or drugs, but it does smell good and his stomach is rumbling, even though it still aches, too.

"Go on and eat it," the man says. "Haven't you ever seen clam chowder before?"

He hasn't. His mom usually makes either chicken noodle soup or beef vegetable. He picks up a spoonful and blows carefully. Meanwhile, the man sits down at the table and takes out his pipe. He packs it expertly and lights it, sending a sweet tobacco scent into the air. The smell makes the boy think of his grandfather, and he relaxes slightly and takes a bite of soup. Thick and milky and salty all at once. His rumbling stomach yearns for another bite and then another.

"What kind of boy doesn't know his own address?" the man muses in between puffs of his pipe. "How old are you?"

"Eight."

"At least you know that. Didn't you have to learn your address in kindergarten? In case you got lost?"

The boy remains silent.

"My grandson had to learn his address in kindergarten," the man continues. "They gave him a red ribbon for it. It said: Hooray! Gregory Knows His Address. Can you believe that? A special ribbon for knowing your own damn address?"

The Sadness of Spirits

"You have a grandson?"

"Yeah, he's a little older than you, and probably smarter, too. He doesn't get lost in the woods. And he knows what clam chowder is."

"What are your dogs' names?"

The man moves his pipe to the edge of his mouth and talks around it. "The black one is Jake. He's a guard dog. And the other one's Molly. Come here, Molly." He bends down and the velvet-haired dog comes running to him. "Go and visit the boy." He glances up at the boy. "You wouldn't happen to know your name, would you?"

"Chet."

"Good. Go and visit Chet."

The dog trots over, and the boy rubs her ears. "She's a very nice dog."

"Of course she is. One of the best."

They sit quietly, the man smoking and the boy alternating between petting the dog and eating his soup. He knows his mom would object to touching an animal while he's eating, but she's far away and her opinion is a distant law that doesn't apply here. When the boy finishes, he places the spoon in the bowl and tries to stand, but the man rises quickly. "I'll get that for you. You have an ugly set of stitches there."

The boy nods and hands him the bowl.

"Do you mind telling me what happened?"

If the boy were older he would tell the man it's none of his business, but he is eight years old and the weight of adult requests is forever upon him, even if the adult also happens to be a murderer or kidnapper living in the woods. "I had surgery," the boy replies. "To remove a nail."

The man sits back down at the table. "How did you get a nail in your stomach?"

The boy swallows hard. It sounds so silly to say it out loud. "I ate it."

"You ate it?" The man leans forward slightly, eyebrows arched. "Why would you do that?"

The boy shakes his head. He can feel tears forming in his eyes, but he blinks them back. Boys don't cry, especially if they want to be firefighters like his dad, but where is his dad?

"Come on now," says the man. "Don't sit there and cry." But this only makes it worse, and the boy can feel the tears running down his face, one of the least masculine sights of all.

"Well, I'm sure you learned your lesson," the man says. "There's not much to be gained from swallowing a nail."

There is much to be gained, and the boy can see it all laid out in his mind: the strength of each item, the weight that makes him a bit more present if only to himself. He wants to tell the man about vampires and how they gain strength from people and people gain strength from cows and pigs and chickens, but the man wouldn't believe him because no one really believes what the boy has to say. They think he's making up stories or "telling lies," as Uncle Rob might say.

The man stands up and stretches. "I can't say I didn't do stupid things in my day. What do you say about getting some sleep?"

The boy is afraid to sleep in this place with the man right across the room, but he nods. The man rolls a sleeping bag across the dirt and stomps out the fire, leaving a few coals to dimly light the room. "Good night," the man says, and his voice is disembodied in the darkness.

"Good night," the boy repeats and settles onto the cot, his mind awake and running in circles, his abdomen a strange and foreign landscape of pain.

The man is up before sunrise, making coffee, waking the boy with his movements. He encourages the boy to eat breakfast, and the boy tries to hobble off the cot and sit at the table, but the pain seems to bend him in half, and as much as he tries he can't hide it. "What's wrong with you?" the man asks, staring at him from above a steaming cup of coffee. "Stitches don't hurt that much."

"Just stiff, I guess." The boy can't bring himself to mention the buttons, the bark, the pebbles.

Once the sun rises, the boy makes his way to the makeshift front porch, which is nothing more than an aluminum overhang with a rickety rocking chair. It hurts to sit and it hurts to rock, but the boy forces himself to do it anyway so that he doesn't draw any more attention to himself. The mean dog watches him closely, and the boy wonders what would happen if he tried to run. Would the dog chase him down and tear him to bits?

He decides not to experiment.

Eventually, the man drags a chair out and joins him outside. He talks about his hunting trips, about how he's gone to Colorado and Montana and seen mountains and deer bigger than anything you would ever see in these parts. The boy pictures these places as the man talks and wonders if he will ever get to experience anything as fantastical as the man describes.

He wonders how Tennessee fits into this landscape, if it's near or far, closer to Ohio or Montana.

The man doesn't ask the boy many questions, but still the boy finds himself talking more than he imagined, telling a little about his friends, about his dad, who is the strongest man he has ever met and a firefighter, too.

"I imagine your dad is looking for you right now."

"I hope so," the boy says, "but he may have moved away."

The man says nothing to this, and the afternoon wears on. Pain distracts the boy more and more. Sharp aches stretch across his abdomen, and he feels weak and unfocused. Occasionally, he catches the man looking at him carefully, and it makes him uncomfortable, as if he's being assessed, as if he's being judged.

He's the boy without a dad close by.

He's the boy nobody will look for.

He's already said too much.

And it's then he realizes the brother in the pickup truck never came. There is still light, but it's fading rapidly, and the old man is inside cooking dinner, maybe another can of soup.

Then what will happen?

His dad wasn't really specific about what crazy people in the woods would do, but the boy knows enough from watching movies to know that people could be hung by their feet, stabbed with knives, chased with chain saws, or poisoned through food.

His mind is a blur of scattered thoughts and shooting pain and dizziness, and he considers potential sources of poisoning—maybe the soup, maybe the water. And there is low ground and bushes and brush, and most brush is below a man's vision. Boys are short and fast and invisible, and he has a plan. He has always had a plan even if it failed the first time. One dog. Two dogs. The mean dog might bite him, but the brother hasn't come, isn't going to come. Maybe there is no brother and no town, and the boy is staggering to his feet and moving to the edge of the clearing even though the mean dog is growling. Then he is in the brush, the brush surrounding him, and he pulls himself together despite the splitting pain in his side, and he is running, running through the brush as fast as his legs will take him.

The dogs are barking in the distance. Two dog voices rage in the air, but they are growing distant. They aren't following him.

The boy collapses beneath a tree, breathing heavily, his abdomen a long rip where his stitches had been, and he is bleeding. He closes his eyes because there is nothing to see anyway: darkness, the moon, one of many summer nights to come in a young boy's life.

He tries to think about where he is, but there is only a dream of a search party in shades of black and yellow stretching across the woods, looking for him, but not seeing that he's right there. And he's searching for his dad, but his dad is watching TV. His dad packed a suitcase, two suitcases, and left and didn't say goodbye.

It's not the boy's fault. None of this is his fault.

Dogs are barking and they are part of the search party, but they scare him and he begins to crawl deeper into the trees. He imagines himself as a snake, only he is dripping blood and he has lost his dad's Swiss Army knife. The old man may have taken it, and he begins to cry at yet another thing he has lost.

The boy closes his eyes: he is a battery.

He forces his eyes open: he is a battery being drained.

How did he become a battery? What is he supposed to do?

His mind burns and forces him to think through these questions again and again, a repetition he needs to stop, but can't. When he turns on his side, he feels liquid ooze from his abdomen and he imagines blood, battery acid. He doesn't have the strength to look down.

Overhead, birds soar and the sun rises, stark and solid. *Save them*, he thinks, and his thoughts are with the birds.

Save me, he thinks, and his thoughts are with himself.

He is falling deeper and deeper into himself. The boy closes his eyes against the sun and does not move. His heart is hammering in his chest, and it is his. He owns it. His lungs rise and fall with air, and they are his. He owns them. He's never thought about it before, but his arms are his and his legs are his, and there is something inside his shell of a body that looks through his eyes and what it experiences is entirely its own even if it is invisible.

Sometimes this invisible self shifts away and the black threatens to return, but he fights it off. He likes this new version of himself, weighted down and present even if no one else can see it. He imagines the bark and buttons and pebbles, and he can't see clearly. Maybe he never could. The dogs are barking, though. The dogs are moving closer and closer, their voices rising high into the sky, and there is another voice calling his name, Chet, Chet, Chet, and it is a single word, poised and ready to be found.

Aching in the Grass

He found her aching in the grass. He was only a mailman and had never encountered aching in the grass before, but there it was, undeniable and sad. He stood beside her, leaned toward her pretty, mournful face, and asked, "Is everything all right?"

She focused her eyes on him, blue eyes, squinted versions of the sky. Around her head, blades of grass and dandelions stirred. "I'm all right," she said. "Just thinking."

She wasn't just thinking; she was aching, too. He could feel it rising up from her in waves, a heavy presence. And she had picked an odd spot to ache. Right out in the middle of her front yard where everyone could see. There was no shame to this woman, but maybe shame wasn't necessary when there was ache.

He continued to stand there. The mail weighed heavy against his shoulder, but when confronted with aching in the grass, he felt he should stay and try to assist. "Is there anything I can do?" he asked.

"No. I'll be all right."

"Are you sure? I can help you up."

"I don't want to get up. Do I have any mail?"

He sifted through his bag. "You have a catalog," he said. "And a Valpak."

She sighed and her eyes moved away from him, following the line of a nearby tree, up and up, across the branches where a bird was flapping its wings, ready to take flight.

"Do you want me to leave your mail here for you?" he asked.

"If it's more convenient."

He gingerly placed the catalog and the Valpak beside her and stepped away. Words formed in his mind, meaningful words that might make her ache subside, but even as they formed they flitted away. Words were just words, and besides, he didn't know how to go about stitching them together, turning them into something hopeful and true.

That night the mailman's dreams were haunted with ache. Images of forests and his father's eyes and cold water were woven together with threads of black. His memories were turned over, given back to him in darker form, and he awoke breathing fast, thankful to see that his wife was still sleeping beside him, undisturbed. When he listened hard, he could hear the soft snores of his son down the hall.

He knew he should get out of bed, go for a walk, and shake these images away, but he couldn't move. His arms and legs were heavy, and his chest felt constricted. The darkness closed in, and the dreams felt as real to him as experience: footsteps down a dark path, dew seeping into his tennis shoes, a girl's hand clutched in his. "If you listen carefully," he had said, "you can hear their voices." And she had nodded eagerly, willing to follow him anywhere.

He pulled himself from the bed, one slow movement at a time, and groped his way down the stairs and out the front door. The grass felt wet against his bare feet, and the streetlights shone down on him. He hovered there for a moment, ache throbbing in his chest, his abdomen, his unsteady legs. His heart beat slowly, resisting its own existence. Overhead the sky was the indigo of early morning, and the stars were the same stars that connected his past to his future. He closed his eyes, feeling wave after wave of sadness washing over him, and then he lay down, overtaken with exhaustion, yet one more victim of ache.

His wife found him there the following morning. "Honey," she said, standing over him in her too-small yoga pants and T-shirt. "Sweetie. What are you doing down there?"

He opened his eyes and glanced at her before fixing his attention on some obscure point overhead. "I'm just thinking. I'm perfectly all right."

"You don't look perfectly all right. Why don't you get up before the neighbors begin to wonder."

"Let them wonder. I wonder about them all the time."

"You're going to get a sunburn," she continued. "It's too hot to just sit outside like this. It's supposed to be in the nineties today."

"Heat doesn't matter. Our ancestors came from Africa." Besides, he was too busy to worry about sunburn. His childhood dog was standing at the edge of their yard, wagging her tail. He could still remember the exact feel of her fur against his fingers, the slight curl of her body as she leaped into the air after a Frisbee. At night she would sneak into his bedroom, a forbidden place, and her breathing would be slow and steady. It would lull him to sleep.

His wife rocked on her feet, heel to toe, heel to toe. "All right," she said as if making up her mind. "I'm going to call the post office, tell them you aren't coming in today."

He didn't answer. He was scratching the dog's ears. He was burying his face in the soft fur of her back, the very best refuge.

The neighborhood came to life. Joggers ran past, their feet pounding against the sidewalk. Dogs barked and strained at their leashes, eager to investigate the man lying prostrate in his yard. Sleepy neighbors started their cars and scrutinized the mailman, to-go coffee mugs in hand.

The mailman didn't notice. He kept his eyes closed. He floated in a golden space. There were his mother's hands, lined with thin wrinkles, composed of fragile birds' bones, tying his shoelaces before taking his hand and leading him out to the driveway to wait for the bus. The bus was bright yellow and had the strangest clean-but-dirty smell he had ever experienced.

His own hands were scratched from reaching into blackberry bushes. He clutched a Dixie cup tightly in his fist. When he put a berry in his mouth, it burst both sweet and sour. "You have to wait until they're ripe," his mother scolded, but she was smiling. She was always smiling until she wasn't, until he found her crying on the couch, her hands drawn over her head.

Rain fell against the car window. It spread in rivulets, and he traced them with his finger, imagining a race. The drops veered apart and then merged together. They became lost in a sea of drops identical to themselves, and he began again with two new drops. Tom Petty played on the radio, and his parents' voices rose and fell.

In the distance, his wife spoke to his son, telling him to eat his breakfast before he could play outside.

Mother. Wife. Son. Parents. The sun burned against his eyelids, and he knew that this day, like other days, would drift into the past, would be tinged gray by memory, the very shade of ache. Even the happy memories. Especially the happy memories.

Small fingers massaged his skin. Cool cream. The sharp tang of sunscreen. "Mom said you'd get burned," his son explained as he coated first the mailman's face, then his exposed neck and arms. "She said you're sick today." The boy stood up and hovered over him. "What's wrong with you?"

The mailman opened his eyes. The sky and wispy clouds were startlingly crisp. "I'm just thinking."

His son sat down beside him, tore up a fistful of grass. "I'll think with you."

"That's not necessary."

"I like to think."

"Why don't you go inside? Dad's busy right now."

The boy sighed but sensed the seriousness of his father's tone. Once the mailman heard his son's footsteps fade into the distance, he closed his eyes again. There was the heavy heat of the school gym, the squeak of sneakers, the thud of a basketball. Other boys were sleek machines, already sinewy muscle and coordination, but his own feet wouldn't cooperate. He couldn't dribble and run. He couldn't catch. He couldn't even follow what was happening. A passed ball struck him hard, knocking the wind out of him, and his glasses slid off his face, hit the floor with a clatter.

That burning. That intense desire to hurt himself. There had to be a better word for self-destructive rage.

"Can we go to the park later?"

His son was back, and the mailman opened his eyes. "We'll see."

"I like the bigger one. The one with all the slides."

"I know you do."

"I can think with you."

"That's okay. I can think by myself."

"Mom said to bring you this." He set a glass of water down in the grass. It was filled precariously to the top, and some of it splashed over the edge with his son's movements.

"Thank you," the mailman said. "I appreciate it."

His son stood beside him for a second and then hurried back to the house. The mailman focused his attention on the surrounding trees, the sky overhead. He knew he should probably get up, do some chores, but standing up would involve too much effort. His aching body simply wouldn't hold him.

Darkness blanketed him. His son had returned, this time with a sun hat. "Mom said sunscreen might not be enough," he explained and put the hat right over his father's face. The mailman exhaled, and his breath was returned to him as a hot fog. "Thank you," he said, and his voice came out muffled.

He couldn't hear if his son stayed or went, but it didn't matter. He was following the forest path, and his hand was intertwined with the girl's and his dog's ghost trotted behind him and perhaps there were other ghosts, ghosts he wasn't ready to think about. "Sometimes you can hear the voices," he told the girl, and mostly he was lying although he wished it were true. "They speak to you when you drift off to sleep at night and tell you about your life's path."

"Sure," she said laughing. "So now you're psychic? You're communicating with the other side?"

"Wouldn't it be cool if I could?"

They had been drinking earlier at a party with all his friends, and he still felt a slight buzz as he walked through the tall grass feeling the dew seep into his tennis shoes. His friends were fun to spend time with, and the mailman's memory veered to their bonfires, their adolescent jokes, but he couldn't remember those details clearly—or at least not in the way he remembered the path.

Cross the bridge. Turn right where the trail forks. Stay out of the pricker bushes. Watch to make sure your pole doesn't get caught in the trees.

He was constantly catching his pole in the trees, losing his line in the bushes across the stream, and his father always shook his head, told him to cut it off and start again. "Don't cast so far," he said. "Pay attention to what you're doing."

The sunlight came down in soft slants during those afternoons. He kept an eye out for the glinting bodies of trout rushing through the tiny rapids.

In the dead of night, the path was shadowed, a haunted version of itself. The girl's hand tightened around his, but he led her forward. Up the hill. Onto yet another bridge that overlooked the deepest part of the stream. He didn't know how deep, but he didn't care as he leaned over the edge and peered down into the ripples. "It's creepy here," the girl said, but he ignored her. He wanted to fling himself into that water. He wanted to lose himself forever.

His father's funeral was still a bodily memory. His eyes sore from tears. His numb legs carrying him across the floor as he moved from guest to casket and back again. His throbbing head sending shocks of pain all over. Slate-gray clouds moving over an open grave that was unreal, unreal. But here by the stream his father's presence seemed returned to him, even if it was only through his imagination: voice, smile, the arc of his arm casting a line, his father refracted a hundred different ways.

He could still feel it now, an ache that swam the rivers within him, easily recalled, as natural as breathing.

There was movement beside him. The mailman removed the sun hat and opened his eyes. His son was lying faceup in the grass, his hand on his forehead to shield his eyes. "What are you doing?" the mailman asked.

"Resting with you," his son replied. "Until you feel better. It's too late to go to the park."

The sun was sinking toward the horizon, and the mailman wondered what had become of the day. He turned toward his son, studying the way his hair fell in dark wisps across his forehead and his eyes solemnly followed the clouds overhead. People talked about childhood innocence, but the mailman knew there were serious thoughts taking place behind those eyes, workings of great gravity that would be mulled over again and again.

He put his hand on the boy's shoulder, so small beneath his palm. "When you're older," he said, "this day will hurt you, and you need to let it."

The boy nodded, eyes wide, and the mailman returned his attention to the sky, watching as the sun faded away and the first stars appeared. They would never grow old, those stars. He could watch them forever.

The following day he returned to his postal route. He thought he might talk with the woman aching in the grass, but the yard was empty and her car was gone. That was just as well. He imagined ache spreading all over the neighborhood like a disease, people suffering silently in their homes or more publicly in their yards, and then he dug through his mailbag, removing two bills and yet another catalog. The envelopes were brilliant white, and the paper was crisp against his hands. He shut the mailbox with a satisfying thump and moved on to the next house and then the next, thankful for how some days could feel illuminated, thankful for how the responsibilities of the moment could only lead him forward.

These Clouds, These Trees, These Fish of the Sea

I am told there is peace in loaves of bread, and so I kneel as I measure—flour, baking soda, sugar—and I stand to pour batter into aluminum pans. I wait, hands pressed together, praying, praying that my bread will somehow rise. I count down minutes, seconds as my teacher, Hilary, passes by and squeezes my shoulder. "I'm sure it will be wonderful," she says.

Wonderful, I think, and the word falls hollow. Fear spreads through my stomach like a fish.

Deep in my nasal cavities I smell sulfur. There is a devil within me, and I am its vehicle.

The bread is dry and overcooked. Even though Hilary smiles as she tastes it, I know she is secretly convulsing. When I get home I throw the bread away and pour a tall glass of wine.

"How was class tonight?" my husband, Miles, asks as he flips through the TV channels. There's nothing on TV. There's nothing to talk about besides cooking, the garbage that needs to be taken out, the bills to be paid. He doesn't make eye contact.

"It was class," I say. "I did nothing productive."

"Then why do you keep going?"

"I'm learning," I say. "I'm making progress."

By morning my head is a slow swelling leading from my sinuses to my forehead and deep, deep within, throbbing, throbbing, and the morning sun is bright and I drink my coffee slowly, breathing in and out, in and out. Often breathing exercises are the only thing that will help with the pain. One breath in. One breath out. The day must go on.

I dress in pure brown and tie my hair back in a ponytail. I wear red lipstick, sharp and distinctive. I don't carry a gun, but I wish I did.

The first perpetrator is a woman walking a dog.

She wouldn't normally be noteworthy, but she drops a plastic water bottle in the vegetation, allowing it to nestle among the endangered plants of Presque Isle State Park, Erie PA's rare peninsula. I stare at the bottle, hardly believing my eyes, and then I begin to follow her. It takes only a minute or so to catch up to her, but in that time she also manages to drop a breakfast sandwich wrapper and a paper napkin. She is shedding trash like some sort of litter snake, and all I can think is that we have garbage cans for a reason and my head is killing me.

"Hey," I say when I get close enough. "Littering is prohibited on park grounds."

I am a small woman with a big voice. She jumps and clasps her chest, a damsel in distress, and I try to hold back my irritation, which is profound. "I found your water bottle," I say. "And your wrapper."

"I'm sorry," she says. "They must have slipped out of my hands."

Her eyes are defiant, daring me to call her a liar, and I sigh. It's so easy not to litter, and yet I find trash everywhere, invading the natural beauty of this place. Why don't people know how to leave a good thing alone?

"I'm giving you a warning," I say. "Don't let me catch you again."

The woman glares at me, and I get the sense that her dog is doing the same. It's a dachshund, shambling along on spindly legs, its pudgy stomach close to dragging on the ground. I hate dachshunds. I hate people who are too lazy to use a garbage can. My chest tightens, but instead of berating her, I force myself to imagine bread. Bread tucked under a towel. Bread slowly yielding to the dancing yeast within.

Without another word, I turn on my heels and walk away. I hope her dog gets hit by a car.

For my lunch hour I stroll along the beach, taking in the waves, the breakers that protect the peninsula from erosion, the endless lake beyond. So much of this place is carefully orchestrated to make sure it breaks down slowly, a deterioration people can process. Overhead the clouds are white and puffy, and I name their shapes—cow, mountain, tiger shark—as they pass by. I call Miles, but he doesn't answer the phone, and I press a hand to my achy head. I continue to name the clouds: cactus, bear, Danny, Danny, Danny.

Words are supposed to have power, and I once used them like a summons, but now I can't put my heart into them. I have only these clouds, these trees, these fish of the sea.

Often the best meals are created from opposites. This is what Hilary tells us as she reveals the secrets of fine cooking. Sweet and sour. Pork and pears. Applesauce and potatoes. "Your own experiences can also be a pairing," she says. "In that way you can own them."

She invites us to think of the saddest experience we have ever had, and then she goes around the room asking us to share. I suppose this is the therapy part of the class, and I listen as people talk about kids turning to drugs, kids falling in with bad crowds, kids doing any number of things that are wrong and might affect their futures. Kids. Always kids, those little heartbreakers. I listen and I don't know how to feel. All my life I have been able to pinpoint my emotions; I have prided myself on being self-aware, but now I am in a new place where everything is turned upside down. I sympathize with these ordinary tragedies, but I also feel tired. There is a hard lump in me that can't be penetrated.

I haven't thought about what I want to say, and so when it's my turn I hesitate for a moment. "You don't have to share," Hilary says. "Sharing is optional."

The other participants turn toward me. They are mostly women in various stages of their lives, and I imagine that regardless of their life experiences, they are united in their judgment of me. I am less than. I am the woman who must be blind. And I am in their therapeutic cooking class.

"It's all right," I say. "When I was in high school I took a childhood development class, and we had to take care of an egg. You know, one of those hard-boiled eggs that you draw a face on and pretend it's a child. Mine had a big smile, and I also drew it a tie. Anyway, I dropped it and failed the project." I shrug. "That was a pretty sad day."

The other women stare at me, unsure if I'm crazy or mocking them, and I feel like I should add more, but the words are no longer there. Instead, I see the egg on the ground, cracks radiating from its broken middle. I set it on top of the car so I could get my bag out. I turned my back for only a minute.

One minute. The shortest longest space of time that ever was.

I'm worried someone is going to ask a question, probe a little deeper, but luckily Hilary turns to the next person, asks her to share, and I stare into my lap. I wonder what a broken egg can be paired with to make it better. My first kiss? My first high school dance?

When I look up I see one of the women watching me. Her hair is fine and gray, and she is wearing big grandmotherly glasses despite the fact that she is probably too young for them. She smiles slightly when she catches my gaze, and I smile back, reflexively. She's probably seen me on the news. She knows that an egg is not just an egg, and she wants to know more.

She won't. Not tonight. I work alone, stirring sweet and sour sauce, concentrating on each swipe of the spoon, hoping that the meditation of meals will transport me to a state of mind that is far, far away from my own.

The following day I am out on the water with Clark, my boating partner, conducting random safety inspections, ensuring that boaters have all the necessary safety items: flares, lights, life vests for everyone on board. For the most part, the inspections go well. The people are polite. They have what they need with a few exceptions. The September sky is blue, and my mind drifts to memories of Miles. We first dated under a September sky. We got married under a September sky.

The cool air brings back sensations of peach picking, drinking white wine.

I am remembering a place where Danny is not, and the realization startles me. Just like that, he is back: swimming in his wading pool, pulling his dinosaur hood over his eyes and pretending to roar, scattering Legos across the living room floor for us to step on.

I close my eyes against the sunlight and wonder what this means. Can a mother truly forget? Is there a part of me that can exist separate from grief?

"Are you all right?" Clark asks. "Is it another headache?"

I feel a surge of affection for this man who would think to ask about my well-being. We've worked together enough for me to confide to him about the pain that rattles me, the way I often can't sleep at night. He is sometimes slow and clumsy, a dangerous combination on a boat, but I don't mind. "No," I say, forcing a smile. "I was just thinking."

I turn my attention to the water, the waves that move as if guided by a hand, catching the sunlight and shredding it into a million sparkling shivers. There are sights that will comfort you if you let them, that allow you to feel as if there is something more than what meets the eye. I remember a story my dad once told where he asked his great-aunt if there was a god and she pointed to the autumn trees, the fall sky, and said how could there not be?

How could there not be? How could there be? There are so many contradictions.

"Hey," Clark says, interrupting my thoughts. "My girlfriend just sent me a text saying she's dropping off my lunch. Do you mind if we go back to shore?"

I don't mind, and a few minutes later I'm waiting as the boat's motor thrums beneath me. Clark's the kind of person who can't pick up a lunch without saying hello, inquiring into the other person's day, and I have time to kill. I think about the cooking class and what we might prepare next. I think about the dish that might hopefully be good enough to bring home to Miles, the dish that might make him smile and set him talking.

That's when I spot an aluminum fishing boat resting too low in the water and think: people would ruin a moment like this.

The boat is propelled by a small motor, and though it's moving, it's not going especially fast. Still, Clark could spend a small eternity talking to his girlfriend, and who knows what kind of she-nanigans these people are trying to pull on the lake. I weigh the op-tions and decide to approach them alone. It's against the rules, but as far as I'm concerned rules are arbitrary. Nothing ever follows a plan, so why should I?

I pull up next to the boat, flash my badge, and list the items I need to see. Already I can tell the boat is over its weight limit. Three aging men with hair in various shades of gray and white and mottled in-betweens have positioned themselves on exactly one fishing chair and two upturned fishing buckets. Dried blood stains the boat's floor, and a listless fish floats in the one bucket that is right side up.

"You don't have any right to search our boat," the man on the chair says. "Why don't you mind your own business?"

"I have every right to search your boat." I keep my voice low and contained as I always do in situations like this. Overhead, a seagull swoops and swerves. Beyond us, the lake stretches like a silent goliath, and I imagine it consuming these men, their bodies becoming yet more debris for us to fish out.

"Why don't you pretend like you didn't even see us?" The man grins to his buddies. "Let us go on our merry way."

"There's no need to make this difficult. I just need to see your flares, your lights, and your life vests."

"What if we don't have life vests? What if we said we were just going to swim to shore?"

They speak the language of measured ignorance I grew up with: Boys who defied teachers and came to school in the orange and camo of their morning escapades. The male patrons of the diner I worked at as a teenager while saving up money for college. "What are you going to do after you graduate?" they asked me as they smoked cigars and cigarettes and drank cup after cup of coffee.

"I'd like to go to college and major in biology," I said, all honesty.

"Right," they said and laughed. "Someday you'll know what women are good for."

I see those men now in the presence of these fishermen, and the anger of those afternoons waiting tables rushes back, makes my hair stand on end. I stay calm, though. I keep my voice low and collected. "If you don't show me your life vests right now," I say, "I'll have to write you a ticket."

"Write us a ticket, then," the man says. "We don't have life vests."

I pull out my tablet and pen. "Can you give me your name, please?"

"Simon," says the man to the laughter of the others. "Simon says leave us alone. Why don't you run on home where you belong?"

"I need your real name please." I wish Clark was here, but at the same time I don't. I don't want him witnessing this ridiculousness. I don't want him to immediately take control of this situation just by virtue of being a man.

"I'm giving you two seconds," I say, making eye contact with each and every one of them. "Then I will be writing you an additional ticket just for being difficult."

"She's going to punish us more." The men laugh. "She's going to write another ticket."

I close my tablet. I'm done trying to write these assholes a ticket. "Fine," I say, which according to Miles is a dangerous word, the most dangerous of them all. "I'll be finding your bloated bodies washed up on shore, then. Your wives and I will dance on your graves."

They are quiet, stunned by this unexpected insult, the bitterness in my voice. Then, as if in slow motion, the leader of the group leans forward and spits directly in my face.

I am in the closet, my wine glass nestled on the floor, and I am going through box after box until I find my old paints and canvas. I have never been spat on before, and in retrospect I think I handled it well. While the men laughed, I slipped my hand into my sleeve and wiped away the spit, being careful not to make any contact. Who knows what kind of diseases a spitter might carry? Then I took down a description of the boat and the three men in it to pass on to the authorities. I said nothing. Why waste words on a lost cause?

Then I went home and poured myself a large glass of wine. Miles raised his eyebrows, but I ignored him. He's never approved of my drinking, even though I like a glass only every once in a while, mainly on the days I've been spat on.

Most of the paints are dried up, leaving me with canary yellow, lime green, and sky blue, despicable colors, but I guess they'll do. I carry the paints back downstairs, spread them around me on the kitchen table, and pick up a brush.

I have no idea what to paint. While I've always enjoyed art and taken some painting classes here and there, I've never considered myself especially creative. That link between the heart and the canvas that some people seem to possess has never existed in me. I float in my own lonely cloud.

I begin with yellow. I paint a canary-yellow oval and begin filling it in. Miles leans over my shoulder, tracking my progress. "What's that supposed to be?" he asks.

"I don't know yet." I open the green, try blending the two colors together. I'm left with a very rotten mess.

"Why are you doing this?" he asks.

"I just feel like it." I don't see why I have to explain myself, especially when we once called ourselves soul mates and vowed to *understand* each other.

He sits down across from me and takes a sip of my so-sinful wine. "You feel some strange things," he says.

I don't answer. He has no idea.

The silence falls around us, and I wonder why we don't listen to music anymore. We should pull out our old CDs, hook up the CD player, but I can't bring myself to move or to speak this request to Miles, who is adept with household electronics. As oppressive as the silence is, it's sacred and I need to immerse myself in it even when the less disciplined part of me wants music, singing, dancing.

"How was work today?" Miles asks.

I'm surprised he's asking, but I say, "It was fine."

"There's that word. What happened?"

"Someone spit on me."

"Someone spit on you?"

"He was upset about his ticket." I neglect to mention the wife-dancing-on-his-grave part.

"I don't understand that."

Miles wouldn't understand because he's never been angry, at least not angry in a way I can relate to. He believes time can heal pain. Cooking can erase sorrow. People can accept with dignity what destiny doles out to them. Meanwhile, there is so much that's not to be understood: three men tempting an unpredictable lake without life jackets, a man spitting on a woman who just wants to help, people interfering in a life that isn't theirs. Spitting. Touching. Pushing. Taking.

A little boy could be on the front lawn one moment. The next he could be gone.

A world is a big place, and a little boy could be anywhere. We could construct a map, search all the places, but it would do no good. There are too many rooms, basements, secret places.

And where does that leave us? How do two people move on when a child could still be alive, could still be clinging to thoughts of the past?

The Sadness of Spirits

"Are you going to report him?" Miles asks.

I shrug. "I took down the boat information, but I didn't turn it in. I kind of lost my temper with him. Sometimes I just don't understand why people can't show some respect."

"To you?"

"Not to me." I don't know how to put it, and so I paint grass around my rotten egg. I paint a sky. "I'm not very good at this." And by this, I mean everything.

"You're doing fine. I'm going to start dinner."

"Do you need my help?"

"No. Keep painting."

I listen to his movements in the kitchen, the clattering of spoons and silverware, running water in the sink, and I think there's too much space here, I need to see him. They are wild thoughts that overtake and make my heart skip a beat, but I focus my attention on the egg. I add black magic marker eyes and a wry smile. I add a lime-green tie.

Humpty Dumpty.

Humpty Dumpty with a stomach bug.

All the king's horses and all the king's men. Attendants of a doomed undertaking. Failing to put the pieces together again.

There is too much symbolism in an egg, especially when I pair it with my child. Eggs and fertility and birth and boys growing up with nursery rhymes. All the fractured parts of my life. Once upon a time, parents had as many children as they could stand so that if they lost one there would be a replacement. Broken pieces could be stitched over.

I'm not sure I will ever have a child again.

My first may still be out there somewhere.

This could be a pairing, too: Humpty Dumpty and hope. I could serve it with pancakes and sausages, little breakfast links, but that feels unnatural to me. At heart, I am practical. I know clouds cause rain and all that I love will die. I'm not easily fooled by words like *hope* and *optimism* and *joy* and *brighter tomorrows.*

I am out walking the peninsula. I was supposed to be on boat duty with Clark, but Clark told our supervisor about the spitting incident under the guise of helping me. "You're under a lot of stress," he said. "A break can help." I was told to stay on dry land and check for fishing violations. I am sure more consequences are coming, but not today and today is all I'm concerned about. For once my head feels fine, and I am taking one step after another, enjoying the trees and grass, the quiet that occurs in the slow time after summer and before the cold of late fall and winter.

When I get home, I will turn on the radio and make Miles his favorite meal.

I will take another cooking class. This time not for therapy, but to learn, to make casseroles and breads and soups that are actually edible.

I will protect this park for all it's worth because it's a rare, beautiful thing.

I turn the corner, and my thoughts are interrupted by a familiar man fishing alone. He is one of the men from the overcrowded fishing boat, not the one who spat on me, but his friend. His back is to me, but I recognize his gray hair curling at the nape of his neck, the green John Deere hat with the fishing license hanging off the back, the big blue cooler filled with his latest catch.

I could turn around now and he would never know I was here, but I'm not the kind of person to walk away from my job. I approach him quietly, waiting until the very last moment to speak and disrupt the calm that has descended on me. No matter what I do, it seems, there's always some event that draws me back to the anger that has gripped me.

Not today, though. I focus on the waves lapping against the beach, the birds calling in the trees. The middle of September. A crisp day of blue.

The Sadness of Spirits

"I'm from the PA Fish and Boat Commission," I say, stepping up beside him. "I need to see your fishing license."

He turns and grins wildly when he recognizes me. "You again," he says. "I thought you would have given up after the first time."

I'm not sure why I would give up or where I would go. I'm just as much a failure in other aspects of my life as I am here, but I try not to think about it. Waves, I think. Birds.

He takes his hat off, flings it at me, and I catch it clumsily. I can feel that burning sensation deep in the pit of my stomach, but I push it away and turn the hat over in my hands, reading the license. "Thank you," I say, handing the hat back to him. "Now I'll need to see any fish you've caught."

He studies me, still grinning, and for a moment I think he's going to fight me on this. I will have to wrestle him for the cooler just because he can't manage to show me the one or two fish he's happened to reel in. I'm not slow. I know the fishing hasn't been great around here and there's no way he's over the legal limit.

But he surprises me. "Sure," he says and pushes the cooler toward me. He lifts the lid and inside is one of the smallest perch I've seen in a long time, resting at the bottom of the cooler, its gills moving feebly.

I pull out my tape measure, make my verdict official. "This fish is under the required length," I say. "You're going to have to throw it back."

He continues to smile, and I don't understand. I don't understand malicious fishermen who only need to follow the rules. I don't understand people who slow down in front of yards, scoop up kids, and take them away. I don't understand need. The greed of taking a fish that's too small, a child who isn't yours. The crushing of vegetation. The spitting. The attitude. The voyeurism.

I just want to be happy again. I just want my son to grow up kind.

Still smiling, he pulls the perch from the cooler, drops it on the ground, and crushes it under his boot. I hear the crunching of bones, real or imagined, and the day swims before me. "There," he says, stepping away. "Now maybe it's the right length."

I can't move. I want to rip him to pieces, but I don't have the required strength or claws or sharp teeth. His eyes, his lips are fragile, and I could lunge for them, but the seconds pass by, and he laughs quietly while the fish rests silently on the ground, its organs crushed, its eyes blank.

There are two ways I can go here, and I feel that everything hinges on this moment.

I step forward and it's not the man I go for, but the fish. I lift its broken body carefully, balance it in my hands, and walk to the edge of the water. In the distance, the lake meets the sky and it all fades together, the edges brushing, completing each other. I take a deep breath, then another, allowing myself to fade into this place that is both beyond and inside me. I think of Danny. I think of all the memories I'll never have and all the hopes I'll never see fulfilled, and I hope that above all he'll learn to find a tranquil place of his own and dwell there. Then I lower the fish into the water, say a silent prayer, and set it free.

Dolls

Gasoline from the back shed. A spool of twine. It is a ritual burning straight from the grand history of ritual burnings. The girl stakes sturdy branches into the ground, assembles piles of twigs at their base. Each Barbie is easy enough to tie—she doesn't put up a fight with those artfully pointed arms and legs; her dazzling smile never wavers. It takes a few minutes for the twigs to catch fire. They're still a little new, a little green, but the girl stacks them into small tents, tucks bits of dried leaves between them. She blows the match carefully, her breath a shiver of molecules she can't begin to understand, and the flame quivers and glows.

Jessica. Samantha. Rachelle. The Barbies have names and narratives she has spent years of her life perfecting. Their legs melt first, the outer rubber of skin giving way to a harder plastic beneath. The flames swallow clothes, the bathing suits that serve as the undergarments of each carefully clad doll, and they only grow bigger. Faces melt, and hair melts, and the smell of burning plastic is sickening.

She has to look away, and that's when she sees her dad, poised near the garage door, extension ladder in hand. His mouth opens and closes, and then he's taking big steps to the coiled hose, unreeling it across the yard. Water sprays down on the Barbies, but not soon enough to save them. "You could have set the whole goddamn yard on fire," he's yelling. "You could have caught yourself on fire. What the hell were you thinking?" His eyes fall on what's left of the Barbies. "What the hell?"

The interrogation begins at roughly quarter after five when her mom gets home from work. They sit her down at the kitchen table and line up the charred remains of Jessica, Samantha, and Rachelle on a newspaper beside her. "This is a very unusual thing to do to your dolls," her mom begins. "Why exactly did you decide to set them on fire?"

The girl shrugs. There really isn't an answer for a question like that.

"I remember when I was your age," her mom says, "my friends sometimes destroyed their toys. Maybe it was a kind of rebellion? Maybe they were suggesting they were too old to play with their toys? I don't know. I never did it myself."

Her dad nods toward the Barbies. "Most people would just pop off their heads."

"I guess what I'm saying is that this is normal," her mom says, "but your method. It's a little sadistic. Why did you have to tie them to stakes?"

The girl considers this question, answers carefully. "It seemed more respectful than stacking them in a pile."

Her parents exchange glances. "But why fire?" her mom asks.

Heat is essential. That's what she's thinking. It does this thing with the air where a small section of the world can become hazy and rippled. It can break materials down into their component parts. It can cause them to become other materials entirely. She wasn't sure what she was expecting Barbies to become, but heat. Heat was necessary.

She shrugs. "I don't know."

"Have you been learning about the witch trials in school?"

"I've learned about them, but not right now."

"Is everything all right at school? Is there anything you need to tell us?"

Her parents gaze at her, waiting for an answer. The truth is that everything hasn't been fine at school, and the problem is with the soda machines. They sit there at the end of the cafeteria glowing with that inward light: Coke, Diet Coke, the illustrated cans specked with condensation that would make anyone thirsty, but the machines are off-limits during lunch because of state laws regarding sugars and beverages. She sits there during lunchtime watching those glowing humming machines, and she thinks about all she knows about the underpinnings of reality. The spinning electrons that may or may not be electrons. The energy that can never be fully measured. The vibrations that rise up through every object, living and non, and shape it with a song. Such a strange miracle to exist. Such a strange miracle to exist and to think. *But what do people do with their existence?* They build soda machines.

She can't quite put it into words, but when she thinks too hard in either direction—the arbitrariness of the subatomic world versus the arbitrariness of soda machines—she feels like all of existence is unfolding beneath her feet, and none of it makes any sense.

And soda machines are just the beginning. There are TVs and lawnmowers and her Barbies staring down at her from their perch on a closet shelf.

When her friends ask her what's wrong, she says, "All of this. I don't understand it." And she gestures to all of the cafeteria, the world beyond.

Her friends are quickly growing tired of her.

She is growing tired of herself. Her parents send her to her room right after dinner to think about what she's done, and she lies on her bed, Barbies beside her. She doesn't think, though, because too much thinking is like spiraling into a dark cave she might never escape from. Instead, she remembers her Barbies—Jessica, Samantha, and Rachelle—and the stories she made up for them. She could always invent elaborate worlds in her head, and so the three dolls were best friends who met every Friday night to go bowling and eat dinner. Samantha was in a terrible car accident, and it was Rachelle who nursed her back to health while Jessica dated Samantha's boyfriend, Ken. Samantha forgave her, and later Ken because he lost his leg and his pants no longer fit right. They got married, and both Rachelle and Jessica were her maids of honor.

The girl could almost imagine them into reality. She could almost love them despite their inner plastic.

She turns off her bedroom light and waits until her parents go to bed. Then she gathers the three dolls up in a blanket and carries them outside. She chooses a remote location near the trees and, with a garden trowel, digs three neat graves, rests the dolls inside, and then covers them in dirt. Meaningful words would be fitting because something has been lost here, but she can't find the words. There is only her breath moving in and out, in and out, rustling the invisible air.

The Long Man

You bury a man in the woods behind your house, and he is a long man. Arms and legs like yardsticks. A head heavy as a pumpkin. There is almost-frozen dirt to lift and scoop, and overhead trees hover like banshees screaming silently into the wind, waving their wicked arms. You tense your back muscles and lift. Tense and lift. A long man needs space. He needs depth. You count quietly to yourself. One, two, three, four. One, two, three, four. Four sets of four followed by four sets of four. Four is the number of stability, following the uncertainty of three and the duality of two.

Four by four by four. You count between breaths. You heave dirt as night falls and the long man disappears into shadows, disappears into silence, disappears into the recesses of your mind. A long man dies once when he takes his last breath. A long man dies twice when the last living thought whispers his name.

Your mind will be whispering his name for a long time, in the quiet moments when your hands are submerged in dishwater, in every nightmare you will ever have.

Everywhere there is the long man. His eyes follow you up and down the stairs to the basement, where you do the laundry, iron his shirts as if he'll be back soon to claim them. They follow you to the car, where you buckle in, to the front door as you check the lock, back to the car, back to the door. You feel him beside you as you drift off to sleep at night, legs that stretch farther than yours, a head that rises above you, a chest to curl into.

You pull the curtains at night because the long man is out there, tamped down beneath dirt and now beneath a light layer of snow. You sit on the floor with legs crossed, close your eyes, drawing your energies, those darting substances that exude and intrude, and turn Tarot cards over in your hands. *Please*, you think, and the question drifts away. Vaguely, there is the long man. The long man sitting beside you. The long man opposed to Tarot cards, the negativity they might summon.

Cards are just cards, cardboard and ink.

The long man is a man and a former man with eyes that can find the threads to unravel you. He watches you from across the kitchen table, now, then. His expression is questioning. "What did you do today?" he asks and takes a sip of wine. You turn his words over in your mind, examining them for their true meaning, replaying the acoustics in your head. What did you do? What *did* you do?

To take someone apart piece by piece. To examine their mind for thoughts of you.

You draw the nine of swords: a young woman waking up from a bad dream only to realize she is living a nightmare. Swords hang over her, nine rising up to the ceiling. Nine brutal blades. Nine thoughts to keep you awake at night.

Nine by nine. Eighty-one. Eight plus one. Nine. Three by three by three. The length of a long man minus some. A card is just a card, but you squeeze your eyes shut as you try to drift off to sleep. The bed is cold where the long man should be. It is simply you and an old patchwork quilt.

A woman calls for the long man, and she is concerned. He hasn't come to work. It isn't like the long man to just disappear.

"A trip," you say, "to visit a very sick sister." So little notice. The frantic flurry of plane tickets and reservations.

You curl up on the couch beneath an afghan and listen as the furnace kicks on, then off, on, then off. One, two, one, two. You open a book and find you can finally focus on the words, sentences lifting off the page into a scene you can immerse yourself in, no longer picturing the long man in khakis and a white shirt and a tie, smelling of the cologne you chose for him, moving through his office, a series of chemicals that have nothing to do with you: dopamine, serotonin, oxytocin, chemicals that once moved for you, chemicals that are no more. You don't have to imagine all the ways he might compare you with others and find you lacking.

Later, you spread the Tarot cards before you, the warmth of your hands transferring to the cards. The eight of swords: a woman tied and blindfolded, surrounded by a circle of upright swords. The card of entrapment. The card of self-imposed restriction.

Fear curls in your abdomen. It smokes out and up, a vapor you can almost smell. Beneath the patchwork quilt, you add the digits of the alarm clock, multiply, subtract.

The next day you receive flowers, a sympathy card. You pin the card to the refrigerator and study it for a long time. Each letter seemingly floats above the white backdrop, sadness on snow, a long man in the yard, fingers curling with cold.

The long man's mother calls. He hasn't been returning her emails.

His friends call. Does he want to go out on Friday?

His boss calls again. Why isn't he at least answering his cell phone?

You stop picking up the phone and count the messages: one, two, three, four. Stability hovering on dissolution. There are shirts upstairs that are his and pants and shorts and underwear and socks. You move from the closet to the dresser to the bathroom where his toiletries are kept. He has left you. He was never really with you, his mind a wilderness where you stumbled and fell and searched and could never quite find what you were looking for.

And he looked into you as if he could see everything.

Handful after handful, you carry his clothes down into the basement, where you pile them up beside the ironing board. Spray the shirts with cold water. Smooth the fabric, one stroke, then two. One sleeve. Two sleeves. Fold and repeat. The long man takes shape through his shirts, tall, precariously thin, and you remember holding your head to his chest at night, listening to his slowly beating heart, his breath moving in and out. Fear rose up in you then, just as fear rises up in you now. There is so much that can go wrong in a long man. So many ways to suffer: skin cancer, pneumonia, ulcers, heart disease, stroke, leukemia, meningitis. You read every medical book you could get your hands on, and then scanned his body relentlessly in bed, in the shower, as he moved through your line of vision while putting on socks and pants and his shirt.

You pick up one dirty shirt and wrap it around you, taking in the smell. Then you choose another and another, shirts piling up on your shoulders, keeping you warm, your hands shaking.

You pull the five of swords before breakfast: a vicious man poised with a sword as other people retreat. The card of tension and betrayal. Victory at all costs.

At midafternoon, you draw the hanged man: a smug-looking man hanging by one foot. Relaxed indecision. Defiance.

You draw the sun. You draw the fool, that thoughtless young man and his bounding white dog. You draw the high priestess, the keeper of intuition and the dark arts.

Again and again you draw the cards, but they seem to make less and less sense. Outside there is the long man and inside there is the furnace kicking on and off, and as much as you try you can't force these cards into any kind of logical narrative. Panic drifts up your legs, settles into your chest. You take the cards, shuffle again.

The four of cups. A young man meditating on three cups while a mysterious hand extends a fourth from the sky. You add it to the line of cards.

If the long man were here, he would grasp your hands and tell you that these are only cards. There are no messages, no mysterious stories to decipher. He would hug you in the same way he hugs you after you wake up screaming, terrified by the dark objects that flutter through your dreams.

The long man is everywhere, but he is not here. You whisper his name in your mind, slowly at first, then faster and faster, trying to reel him back from the place he has gone, but the house is still silent, heavy with pent-up tension.

There is movement outside the window. A meter reader walks past, his vest a blaze of orange. You can never be as alone as you need to be, but you are also too alone. The clock ticks and you gather up the cards, wrap them in their scarf, and try not to think of them anymore.

You bury a man in the woods behind your house, and then you bury yourself above him, stretched out in the snow, snow on top of you, snow falling from the sky to conceal you. Your body is cold, cold, but that doesn't matter because you are whispering the long man's name and watching the clouds make their trek across a slate sky. One, two, three, four. Their movement is slow and soothing, easily countable. There will be more phone calls. There will be police. There will be demands for explanations, and you will think of all the times you traced his footsteps in your head, the panic you felt when you thought of a long man who was only bones and skin, organs and blood. Worry compounded by worry. You would count his heartbeats, hoping for the number to symbolize perfect health, but what that number was escaped you and you could never be satisfied. There was only night and fear's endless ache and the desire for it to stop.

You count clouds and then you count yourself, the long man. One, two, one, two. The clouds scuttle past and you wish you could freeze them, hold on to this moment forever, but the only two who are frozen are you and the long man, and you grasp this duality, the gravity that holds you to him, him to you, one plus one, one times one, one times zero canceling, canceling until you, too, are lost.

Disappearance

The change first occurred as a feeling of vertigo in open public spaces. There was an awareness of the size and depth of the space around her, followed by dizziness, as if she might fall down and lift out of her body at the same time. Her surroundings opened up and every possible sensation flew in: the sunshine, the sound of traffic rushing past, the movement of the wind, the heat.

It was worse when she was outside, walking or jogging down the street that branched away from her house and led into the busier part of town, but it could also happen at the mall or the grocery store or the craft store where she eternally shopped for fabrics.

At first she told herself it was just anxiety. Mild panic attacks, which could happen to anyone. So much had changed in her life. She had moved into a new house, and her husband had moved across the country for work. "We'll see each other for Christmas," he promised her, "and maybe Thanksgiving, depending on the cost of plane tickets."

"Maybe Thanksgiving," she repeated.

"It will only last about a year. Then the company will send me home."

She did her best to be understanding. This was the new way of the world. People had to move far, far away for work. Families had to be flexible and tolerate each other's absence. Military couples had it much worse. Still, the silence of her house at night took its toll on her. Every creaking door and settling floorboard was a ghost, which she believed in somewhat during the day and fervently in the middle of the night. Every strange meter reader at the door or unfamiliar maintenance worker became cause for concern. She circled the interior of the house every morning before she left for work and every night before she went to bed, checking and double-checking and triple-checking every door and window lock, every burner on the stove. Left to her own devices, she was sure she was going to overlook something important.

In her spare time, she read internet articles about how climate change was killing species all across the world, agonized multitudes that people didn't even see because they couldn't be bothered to look up from their phones occasionally. She read about the increasing gap between rich and poor, the new Gilded Age. She followed links to articles about problems in education and education being pointless when machines would eliminate most jobs and about machines that could slam particles together until they broke down into their component parts, which seemed to be nothing, and then formed small black holes that could swallow the earth and the moon and the sun and pretty much everything else whole.

Her breakdown was swift and occurred in her beloved craft store. One minute she was running her fingers across a silky pink fabric, and the next the lights above were boring down on her and the ground slipped out from beneath her feet. One of the teen-age workers, not a big crafter herself, found her there in the aisle, clutching her head in her hands and rocking to and fro.

Her therapist, a slightly judgmental woman with permed hair and big beaded necklaces, prescribed her antidepressants and reg-ular therapy sessions. "It's not unusual for people to feel anxious when they suddenly find themselves alone," she said. "This hap-pens all the time with grieving spouses and single parents whose kids move out of the house."

"My husband isn't dead," she said.

The therapist gave her a long look as if to say he might as well be.

She went to her therapy sessions regularly, but she stopped taking walks and going for runs. The moving traffic and constant sunshine were too much. She took a leave of absence from work. Then she stopped going grocery shopping during the day, instead preferring to slip in and out of the store in the dead of night like some sort of fresh-produce vampire. She ordered her craft supplies online and pretended to be upstairs or dead when the mailman came to the door. She collected all boxes around dinnertime when she was sure her many neighbors would be too distracted to see her open the door and gather her goods.

"Agoraphobia," her therapist said as if she had just termed something new and exciting. "The antidepressants should be helping."

She shrugged. She didn't believe in mind-altering medication. Never had an antidepressant passed her lips.

"We'll just have to increase the dosage," the therapist said. "See if that helps."

"You have to keep taking your antidepressants," her husband said during his one nightly phone call. "Although I do think a lot of it is in your head. You just need to calm down. Do you try doing breathing exercises?"

She held on to the sound of his voice, those waves of sound and reassurance traveling to her from so far away. "Yes," she said. "I breathe."

"Just concentrate on that."

She was quiet. Words hung in her mouth, aching to be released. Could words ache? Could her own lonely ache be the cause of all this drama?

She didn't think so.

"No," he said. "I can't come home now." As if he knew exactly what she wanted to say.

She began skipping her therapy sessions and shutting the blinds during the day, but that only made her feel grim and claustrophobic, and so she took to the internet, browsing home improvement sites and gardening catalogs.

The pieces of her future fence arrived on a Thursday.

Her shrubs, still small, still waiting to be nourished, arrived on a Monday.

And on the days that followed: seeds of every imaginable variety. Sunflowers to stand guard. Petunias to hang from windows and doors. Vines to climb the sides of the house. Dahlias. Marigolds. Cucumbers and zucchini and beans and tomatoes. The more food she grew, she reasoned, the less reason she had to leave the house.

She ordered a vegetarian cookbook.

She built the fence in stages, erecting pieces of it by day in the safety of her garage and then actually building it in the silence of night. If her neighbors wondered about this strange process, they didn't let on. They didn't actually seem to notice her at all. Cars and pedestrians meandered past the house. People went to work and came home. It was, she noticed, unusual for anyone to spend much time outside at all.

Once the fence was done, she felt safe coming out into the shining heat of the day. She planted her shrubs as a kind of second border beside the fence and chose small areas for flower gardens and other areas for vegetable gardens. Day after day she worked, planting more seeds, nurturing the bits of green that arose, the flowers and vegetables that eventually took shape.

Over the course of the summer, her front yard acquired a leafy sort of density, a forbidden-forest kind of feel that only left her feeling safer. She began to wonder why more people didn't garden, if only to escape the world for a little bit.

She soon found she was able to concentrate on just one task at a time. Sound disappeared and there was only sight. The purple petals of her petunias, striped by a bit of white. The pink unfolding head of a climbing rose. Its neighbor, the blue rose, standing by like a kind of lackluster shadow. And when she focused on the sounds of the wind or the call of the birds—crows especially seemed to gather around her house and gossip with each other all day long—the sights of her garden faded from her mind and there was only the sensation of sound moving through her.

She cooked dinner at night and no longer heard the news, which she usually turned on in the background. The pleasure of slicing a squash or simmering a pasta sauce supplanted everything else in her mind. And when smells rose from each pot to greet her, her vision darkened at its edges, as if one sense organ was shrinking back to make way for the other.

The darkness began to infringe on other moments during the day. She would be holding a half-ripened tomato in her palm and realize, vaguely, that she couldn't see the maple that stood on the edge of the yard, or the shrubs, or the fence. Her vision collapsed to a small oval that included her hand, the tomato, and the plant directly in front of her.

She didn't worry about it too much. Vision problems had always run in her family, and she wasn't about to go to the doctor.

Her husband continued to call once a night, but if she wasn't listening for the phone she missed it. "You seem distracted," he said to her when they finally did talk. "And I feel like more and more you don't answer at all. Is everything all right?"

"Everything is fine." She focused on the sound of his voice, the delivery of each word, flung like a rock into a pond where it created ripples. She could see those ripples, moving farther and farther in all directions. They brought to mind galaxies minus the rotation, minus the magnificent spirals.

"Are you listening to me?" her husband said.

"Yes," she replied. "No. My mind wandered for a moment."

Their conversation held all the tension of the usual unspoken questions: Was she having an affair? Second doubts about their marriage? Were there side effects to all the drugs she was taking? On some level she knew she should try to address these concerns, but she couldn't seem to hold all the thoughts together in her mind. When her mind conjured the word *affair* she clearly saw fishnet pantyhose and illicit afternoons in the bedroom or bathroom or kitchen, but none of it had anything to do with her, and explaining this to her husband would take too many words. The sentences would spread out, but then darken before they could be finished.

"I love you," he said, his voice hopeful.

"I love you, too," she said, and that was something she could hold on to.

In her garden, she began harvesting zucchini and eggplant. The oval shrank to a smaller oval and then to a circle of light. Mini binoculars, she thought. Mini binoculars that allow you to see close up. She had to concentrate when she moved the zucchini and eggplant she was picking to the basket by her side. The landscape of her yard moved inch by tiny inch, and it was easy to get confused. She didn't mind, though. Her movements acquired a kind of slowness, as if by compensation. She felt more attuned to the leaves of her plants, the blades of grass, the individual slats of her basket than she ever had before.

The Sadness of Spirits

When she looked in her bathroom mirror at night, she was confronted with a single brown eye, a stretch of skin specked with pores, two nostrils. Features of a foreign body. She viewed them as if from a distance, turning them over in her mind, wondering about the person who lurked beneath their surface before brushing her teeth, carefully, one glistening white pearl at a time.

The tiny details of her house held more and more interest for her, and whole days would go by before she even went outside. Instead, she would sit on her couch or at the kitchen table and look at one spot on the wall, a bit of paint with a slightly ridged texture, or at her coffee mug. Her vision dimmed and she would listen to a passing car. The car would grow silent and she thought: there's so much that person is missing.

At night, the phone rang in the background and she did not rise to get it. She appreciated the way it broke the silence, the music of its summons.

Then she woke one morning and the circle was gone. She floated on a field of black that was like consciousness, but was also something more subdued. The peacefulness of existence without thought. The calm of an eternal meditation. She was aware of her thoughts whirring away, attempting to make sense of this new way of being. Then her thoughts blurred to make way for the calling of a crow outside her window. Then the slow rise and fall of her eyelid, the swish of an eyelash. A muscle twitch. A heartbeat. Another. And another.

Mailman Fantasies

This is where obsession begins: a bag of letters and a mail truck. A man who wears long shorts and sunglasses, who is tan. Tan from the sun. She passes him on the stairs leading up to her apartment, and he speaks in a voice that is authority. "Aren't you going to keep me company?"

She pauses on the steps. She is wearing a red sundress and patchouli musk perfume. Her scent is strong on the air, and he is breathing slowly, making it his. "I can," she says. "How have you been?"

She addresses him as a friend even though this is the first time they've ever spoken. This pleases him, and he smiles slightly as he looks her over through his sunglasses. She knows he is doing this even though she can't see his eyes. "I've been fine," he says. "Do you go to school here?"

"No," she says. "I graduated a while ago. Now I work at the library."

"You're a librarian?"

"A librarian."

He turns this over and his voice is careless, disinterested. "I don't read much," he says. "I suppose I'll be seeing you around."

It is a big world, and the mailman is everywhere. She sees him during her late afternoon walks as she makes her way down the block and around the corner, stretching her legs, thinking. He calls to her when he spots her, leaning away from whatever doorway he is at, locking eyes with her. "Where have you been?"

"Hiding," she says. Always hiding. There is no other way to answer this question. Someday he will want to know where she hides. He will want to see her lair, but not now. These sorts of things take time. They are a slow progression.

She feels his eyes on her as she walks even though he is nowhere in sight.

She runs errands some afternoons. When her car is idling at a corner stop sign, he comes right up to her driver's side window. The summer heat is dizzying, and she leans away from him, farther into the cool of the air conditioner.

"Aren't you going to take a walk with me?" he asks.

"Not today," she says. "Someday."

"I'll hold you to it," he says as the traffic clears and she pulls away, his words in her ears, her face in his sunglasses. How long will he hold the image of her there? she wonders. Will the heat burn it in or melt it away?

During a brief afternoon rain, he pulls his mail truck into the parking lot of her apartment complex. He gets out and stands before her window, staring up at her, the rain pouring off his uniform, drenched and blue.

She leans against the window, a queen, but more modest. The curtains blow past her, and she catches one absently, presses it to her cheek. Neither of them speaks. Slowly, he removes his sunglasses, a promise, a plea. She sees his eyes are like hers: dark and wanting.

On the days when she works, she stands between rows of books, shelving, rearranging books that have somehow gotten out of order. She is neatly dressed in a pencil skirt and pink blouse. She is no one to look at, but men still turn. Her scent follows her throughout buildings, around aisles, past tables, and up the stairs to the second floor where windows overlook the bay.

Her scent follows her and the mailman follows her. She feels his eyes everywhere. She is still stopped by the sound of his voice even though it is only a memory.

The bay is blue, blue and the boats speed past, but all that color is too cool for the vibrating fever within her. She turns away and imagines the pavement, the feet that tread it, and the slow heat that rises in shimmers.

In her dreams, he is selling her towels. "Come here," he says, a pink towel in hand. "I want to wrap you in it."

She lets him, standing completely still as he slips it around her shoulders, pulls it snug in front. "How does that feel?" he asks. "Does it feel the way a towel should?"

She doesn't know how a towel should feel. Her mind is hazy and dark, the way it often is in dreams, and the words won't come. The towel is soft against her skin, and she's aware of creeping warmth, the flush of her face.

"They're on sale," he whispers. "Let me get you a cart full."

She doesn't need that many towels, but she's awake and the towel feels real although she is covered only with her own skin and the thin cotton of her nightgown as it twists around her body. A

The Sadness of Spirits

breeze blows in through the open window, but it is still hot, too hot to keep sleeping.

The night sky seeps through the window, spilled ink speckled with stars, and she thinks, *The mailman is out there somewhere.*

When she is away from the circulation desk, moving up and down the aisles, shelving books, she feels like she is in a dream. Sound stops. Time stops. Only the water moves, waves rippling from left to right, ceaselessly, past the library. In the afternoon the sun beats down on the water, turning it cerulean.

She longs to fall into that water, not to swim but to feel submerged. She imagines her body floating downward, her hair spilling out like a cloud, her eyes slowly adjusting to the water. The sun would reach her with muted rays, illuminating fish and seaweed and her fingers and arms and legs.

Would the mailman find her in that water? Would he even know where to look?

It seems like some sort of telepathy should bring him to her. If he knows her, then he should know about the water, the way it relieves her from the heaviness of each day. She didn't even know how weighty time could be until she came to this town, this library, far away from her friends and family.

She imagines him swimming toward her, still dressed in his uniform. With or without the sunglasses? She can picture him clearly either way. He takes one hand and then the other, but he doesn't pull her to the surface. "Listen," he whispers. "The fish are dancing." And she doesn't see them, but she can hear them, the pitter-patter of a thousand tiny fins flipping through the water, a beautiful synchronized motion.

He is at her apartment now. He is holding a letter, and his sunglasses are firmly over his eyes. "Am I too late for lunch?" he asks.

Her apartment is heavy with heat, and the clock ticks by slowly in the still air. Her body is both dense and light, a woman underwater, and she pulls the door open farther. "No," she says. "You're right on time."

It is an ordinary day. The neighbors are at work or washing their dishes or watching afternoon soaps, but here is the mailman, pressing her to the carpet, his sunglasses folded on her coffee table.

The tree outside her window appears to shimmer in the afternoon light, each leaf burning into the next until it seems the whole tree is afire, simmering beneath a spectacular sun.

She walks with the mailman, behind him, before him as he delivers the mail. He is a planet she is orbiting, a whole terrain of hills and foreign tongues waiting to be explored. People drive past in cars, walk by on foot. Crisped people. She marvels at the way the sun is drying them, the way the heat shimmers off their bodies. There is so much potential for fire. They are walking flames, and they don't even know it.

At her apartment, she presents him with a freezer pop. Blue, which coats his tongue and lips. She longs to bury herself in his blue—tongue, lips, the broad expanse of his shirt—but there is still mail in his bag, and the day is short. Later she asks herself this: How many women are seduced by their mailman? How many of them are overtaken first by the idea of him, then later by his form?

It is an impossible question to answer. Somewhere in the neighborhood, the mailman is moving, slipping from door to door, down alleys, then out into the light, his shoulder heavy with unopened messages.

When she closes her eyes, she can't picture him clearly. Instead, she opens her closet where she keeps her scarves. She runs her fingers across them, drapes the cool fabric around her neck, her skin sensitive to every touch.

The bay is taking on a crystalline quality, like glass. She stands by the window and stares at it, imagining what would happen if the surface cracked and broke apart. Would there be a whole separate reality beneath it? Would it be better or worse than this one?

The mailman is standing to her right. "Look at that," he whispers. "That's a good ice skating surface."

An elderly man is standing to her left. "What's wrong with you?" he asks. "I just asked you a question."

She turns to him. "And what was that?"

"Mystery novels. I wanted to know if you have any new mystery novels in. My wife asked me to pick up a couple."

She wants to tell him to look outside. There are more pressing matters than mystery novels, especially since the bay has turned to glass and he is smoldering. She can see the smoke rising off the shoulders of his T-shirt.

"All right," she says. "I can show you where the new books are, but you have to promise to be careful." And she leads him through the silence, the labyrinth, her dream, her prison, leaving the mailman far behind.

He is seated on the edge of her bathtub, the mailman. The shower is running and he pulls her foot to his uniformed knee. "When was the last time," he asks, "you had a shave this close?" And he reaches for her razor.

"Yesterday," she says. "Never." Time is insignificant now. There are only strokes up and down, white foam giving way to bare skin.

She walks through the library. She walks through her neighborhood. Evening sets in and the air dampens and cools, but still she is buzzing, buzzing. She passes open windows and talking TVs and talking people. Dogs bark in the distance and boys hoot, and everything is ordinary, but also not ordinary. She is ordinary and not ordinary, too. She is two legs and two feet and two arms and one head, and she is on fire. Only the cool evening air makes the heat bearable.

She thinks of the mailman. She wonders if he is also on fire.

She doesn't know his last name even though he knows hers. It seems that names don't matter much in this world.

She knows he dreams of his grandparents' farm in Virginia, a place he used to visit as a boy. He described it to her in whispers past her hair: the white farmhouse with the wraparound porch, the old horse, the acres of corn. She followed him there, temporarily letting his dreams mesh with hers as the two of them meandered down old dirt roads and hid from each other in the corn until the temptation to be together grew and they fell into each other's arms again.

He knows when she slips from his apartment one night and lies out in the grass, her body shaking. He brings her a towel. He says, "You looked cold so I brought you this." He doesn't notice that the towel is too small and hardly covers her thighs. He doesn't notice that she's still shaking, nor does he understand that her trembling has nothing to do with the cold.

They sit together, and she watches the stars while he stares at some point down the road. There's so much that can be said in this moment when she is hot and cold and aching, but she can't bring herself to speak, and he doesn't bother to say anything, and in the silence she knows that despite the time they've shared, they're not truly meant for each other. Someday she'll look back and remember the loneliness of this summer, she'll remember the heat, but she'll have trouble remembering just what was real and what was fantasy.

"We should go inside," he says and reaches for her hand. "You're going to catch a cold."

"I'm already cold," she says, but he doesn't understand what she means. He doesn't see the way the sky is icing over, crackling around the glowing stars, and maybe he doesn't have to. This sky is her sky.

One night after work she sits by the bay and watches as a couple launches glowing lanterns into the sky. They hover for a moment over the water like shimmering jellyfish, and then rise up and up until they look like fiercely glowing stars that shine and then fade.

She wonders what they are celebrating. A religious tradition she's never heard of? An anniversary? The souls of departed loved ones? It doesn't matter. When she watches the lanterns she thinks of love, the outpouring of devotion in the form of fire sent floating, and that's enough.

Two kids are fishing to the right of her, and to the left the mailman is nowhere to be found. The kids laugh and reel in pieces of weed and the occasional fish, and she stands up to get a better look. The water is glass, but the kids are still fishing. Somehow, somehow, there has to be a better world down there. She slips off her shoes and carefully reaches one foot toward the glistening surface, then the other.

She stands on the water, and then begins to walk, her feet sizzling. She doesn't know if anyone sees her and she doesn't know where she's going, but she goes on, beyond the city, beyond the prying eyes of the mailman, hoping to fall through, following the burn of a lantern as it leads her deep into the night.

Winter

More and more there is this: Cecilia wakes to find the edges of her existence turned crystalline and hot. She can't see them clearly, wrapped as she is in an afghan on the couch, but she can feel them slowly closing in on her. They crackle with heat; they reach out with blazing fingers. She wants to reach back, but can't. Who knows what she will find or if she will find anything at all.

She is an old woman, of course, given to moments of forgetfulness and senility. Even she knows she is no longer functioning at her best.

The muted winter light glows gray through the window and snow falls. Snow always falls. It is eternal winter now, the robust summers of Cecilia's youth long gone. She misses them and the way the sun once stretched broad and blue overhead, but somehow this change is fitting. As one season ends, another must begin. Life and time and weather and matter are always passing away, changing form. It doesn't matter that the house is so cold that in some places Cecilia can see her breath. It doesn't matter that the furnace can no longer keep up. Cecilia is far past worrying. So things are, so they must be.

Her habits are carefully timed rituals and she needs to get up and start making dinner, but she doesn't have the energy to lift a hand, much less climb to her feet. She watches the snow fall and thinks, *I can wait an hour or so. There's no hurry.* She lets her eyes fall closed. She allows her conscious mind to give way to whatever lies beneath.

And then there is this: she is a little girl standing in a parking lot, a purple scarf around her neck, her face upturned to the snow-sputtering clouds. The sky is slate gray, and the cold cuts through her jacket and settles deep into her bones. She wants to run, but she stands. Her feet bob up and down. And then the girl turns to Cecilia—the child's eyes meeting the woman's—smiles, and reaches out her hand.

That cold. This cold. That girl. This woman. She drifts in and out of consciousness and can no longer differentiate between the two.

Cecilia's daughter, Diane, comes to get her early in the morning. Diane moves through the house, preparing coffee and a couple of eggs for breakfast, dragging a sweater and coat and thermal underwear from Cecilia's closets. Diane is thick bodied with strong hands and a very determined way of going about things. Growing up, Cecilia never would have imagined that she'd give birth to a daughter like this, but then again Diane has had to adjust to a very different set of circumstances: endless winters, endless cold, an endless life.

"We need to update your furnace," she tells Cecilia. "There's no reason for you to be living like this."

"It's nothing to worry about. I get by." She pauses for a moment to run her hand across the sweater Diane has taken from the closet. It is still soft and pleasing, despite its age. Her husband gave it to her for her forty-fifth birthday, and it's still one of her favorites. They simply don't make sweaters like this anymore.

"Here, this will help you warm up." Diane shoves a cup of coffee into Cecilia's hand. She doesn't make eye contact. "We need to get going or we'll be late."

Diane drives slowly, maneuvering the truck over patches of ice and snow. In some places, it seems like the road hasn't been plowed at all, and Cecilia leans against the window to get a better look. Plow drivers are running out of places to put the snow, and they pass fields where piles of snow stretch higher than the truck. Trees lean beneath the weight of accumulated snow, and single-story homes are mostly buried with cleared sidewalks indicating their existence, leading up to their carefully excavated doors.

"The trees are going to die," Cecilia observes.

"Maybe, or else the hardy ones will survive." Diane keeps her eyes focused on the road.

Cecilia's not sure what survival is worth in this world where leaves are unwelcome, but she doesn't say anything else. It is snowing again, and she tells herself that Diane needs to concentrate even though it seems Diane can do most things with her eyes closed. She herself would not want to drive in this weather, which is mostly why she keeps to herself, knitting and cooking at home, looking through old photographs, living off the contents of the pantry.

She turns her attention to Diane. "How's Jackie?"

"She's fine. She got all As and Bs on her last report card, which we're happy about." Diane pauses for a moment. "She always asks about you."

"She could call me."

Diane says nothing. Apparently, the idea of a phone conversation doesn't warrant further discussion.

At the doctor's office, Cecilia is immediately whisked into the examination room. Not many people need physicians anymore, and she is the only patient. She sits for a moment on the table, and there is that warmth again, burning at the edges of her. She swings her feet, tries to focus on thoughts of her daughter in the waiting room, her granddaughter away at school, but it is hard to concentrate. Snow tumbles to the floor, and she doesn't immediately realize it's only her imagination.

The doctor is young in appearance, although that doesn't mean anything anymore, and he pokes and prods, takes some blood. He has been schooled in a kind bedside manner, as all the doctors have, but that must have been his weakest class because she catches him giving her strange glances out the corner of her eye. Old women are rare. Her visit is a unique opportunity for him.

An hour later—everything is so fast now, she thinks—the results are in and the doctor sits down across from her. "I have good news and bad news," he says.

Cecilia nods. Good news and bad news have gone hand in hand for as long as she can remember.

"The bad news is you have bone cancer," he continues. "The good news is it's very treatable. We can put you on a regimen today."

Cecilia breathes in slowly, breathes out. Sometimes this world she now inhabits is like a dream: always iced and snowy, the cancers that once killed now curable, old age a strange circus act. She doesn't know what to expect from one moment to the next. She doesn't know what to feel.

"Well, I hope that sounds like good news to you," says the doctor. "And if you wait just a moment I can show you how to do the first injection."

The wind seeps through the walls. It curls around her, and she smells snow, that crisp scent of November. There is cement beneath her feet. She is hopping through Oklahoma, and there is a football game in the distance. Maniac Magee, she thinks. Maniac, Maniac, Maniac Magee.

There are moments to stand and moments to run.

The snow sputters down on her. It floats around invisibly in this frigid office.

Once inside the school, she will run cold water over her fingers, slowly warming it so as not to shock her skin. She will sit on the reading carpet as the teacher takes a seat on the beanbag. He will read the story of Maniac Magee, and she will stare out the window at the clouds, imagining all the places she could run to.

She is distantly aware of a vibration. Then. Now. Here. There. It is in the air, wrapped in the embroidery of space and matter and time, but it is also within her. It is the beating of her heart, the mystery of DNA curving around and around, dictating a single destiny. People can preserve life, but they can never define it. To prolong life is to perhaps never know its source.

"What do you say?" the doctor asks. "Are you ready to get started?"

She stares at him. How could he ever feel what she has?

"I don't know," she says. "I'll have to think about it."

His kind attitude diminishes slightly. "These injections will save your life."

"I know."

He is quiet a moment. "You understand that there is protocol involved in declining a treatment?"

She nods. In this world there is always protocol, there are always permissions to get, hoops to jump through. People can never just be. "Let's get started," she says. "My daughter is waiting outside."

The Sadness of Spirits

Again, there is this collapsing: a rush of air so cold it burns, a child's voice whispering of Magellan's fated journey around the world and its sad juxtaposition of discovery and death, the unsettling flip of déjà vu as if she has lived this moment again and again and again. Cecilia presses her face against the frosted bus window and breathes out warmth and memory, a past standing both behind and ahead of her, waiting, waiting to meet her.

The other passengers know enough to draw toward the center of the bus for warmth. They stare straight ahead, wrapped in heavy coats and scarves and hats. A few of them glance toward her, this strange woman who acts as if she's never ridden on a bus before, and it's true. It's been years since Cecilia has boarded a bus and visited the world beyond her comfortable house. She can't see much now. Blurred shapes speed past the window, but still she strains to watch. Reality has always possessed an otherworldly quality for her, as if what she sees is just a thin disguise for a system much more complex, but it's just a feeling. No one gives feelings much thought anymore. Emotion has been reduced to chemicals, hormones, random electrical surges.

She listens to the bus driver announce each stop, the names forming a map that is both distant and familiar to her. When her stop is called, she rises unsteadily to her feet and carries her heavy purse to the front of the bus. The passengers' eyes are on her; she can feel them, but she is careful to stay focused on each slippery step, the salt-splashed tops of her boots.

Outside, the city is a sad semblance of what it once was. Cecilia can remember the days when it was just a small, rural town with a single blinking yellow light at its one intersection, but the population gradually grew as people flocked from up north in an attempt to escape the increasingly brutal winters and people began living longer, extending their lives first with stem cell therapy, then with DNA resequencing. There was the boom time when the buildings stretched fine and stately into the sky and the trees bloomed and restaurants and stores lined the main street, but now overpopulation and cold and scarcity have taken their toll. Still, people hold on, especially since the situation is worse in the slightly more temperate regions further south where the majority of the displaced settled. Poverty and starvation. People huddled together on the streets without enough warm clothes to go around.

Cecilia makes her way down the sidewalk, which is slushy from so many footsteps. "You could have gone anywhere," Diane often tells her as if it is her fault they didn't settle in a better location before the climate shifted. "Yet you just had to stay put."

Diane's right. As a girl, she loved to hop across the map of the United States painted on the school parking lot, her feet taking her from Massachusetts to Oregon and back again, but as an adult she realized none of those faraway places held magic for her. Excitement, she found, was always right in front of her.

Or maybe it was lack of imagination that kept her in the snow. Maybe it was fear. It's so easy to second-guess your motives when you're looking over the span of decades.

She finally locates the building she's looking for, 311 Main, and stops outside on the sidewalk. The siding is dark brown and as drab as all the other buildings on the street. The windows are covered with the customary black thermal curtains to hold in as much heat as possible. The therapist's office is on the third floor, and she feels tired at the thought of all those steps. The office itself is sure to be cold. A chill in the air. Wind gusting through the cracks in the walls.

Her whole body aches, from cold, from malfunctioning cells. Inside, the therapist is waiting to tell her that life is always worth living even when it's dreary, perhaps especially when it's dreary. You never know what the future will hold. The sun could come out any day.

He'll remind her that it's not too late to begin the resequencing. She could feel years younger in a few months.

She continues walking. The cold and long stares from the other pedestrians are dizzying, and she focuses on the movement of her own feet, the sound of her own voice in her head: Maniac, Maniac, Maniac Magee. What was he running from? She doesn't remember. Someone laughs in the distance. A little girl. A little girl spinning in sputtering snow.

The wind slips through the thin parts of her coat, the sweater below, the undershirt she wears. It is a cold like she has never known before, and somehow that is fitting. She doesn't know exactly where she's walking, although she feels like the direction is faintly familiar. A left at the intersection. Wait for traffic to clear. She is gray hair and fine lines and a slow, crouching walk. She isn't even completely off the road before cars tear past her, their passengers leaning close to the windows to get a better look.

The pressure of each step is hard on her knees. Her purse feels like it weighs a ton. Slushy snow splashes onto her pants, and her breath comes hard and ragged.

When she reaches the elementary school parking lot, she has to lean against a parked car to rest. Briefly, she wonders what she looks like: an old woman dressed in a mismatched assortment of old clothes, holding on to a car for dear life. Everything here feels old and mismatched. Many of the cars are actually collages of other cars, parts taken here and there, wherever they can be found. People will drive them for as long as they run.

The elementary school isn't much better. The bricks seem to be crumbling in places, and again the windows are concealed with black thermal curtains. She imagines the kids hunkered at their desks, bathed in dim light, scarves wrapped tightly around their necks, practicing addition and subtraction, phonics and spelling. They aren't allowed outside even for recess, partly because the playground equipment is buried in snow and partly because the frigid temperatures are too dangerous.

Jackie is somewhere in there. Jackie, who always wants to hear about Cecilia's childhood. Jackie, who doesn't stare at her aging face. Cecilia could go inside and visit with her. Who would deny a grandmother time with her granddaughter? They could slip off to the cafeteria or to a quiet table in the library and just talk together. Jackie would tell her about her friends and their games or about the books she is reading or about the questions she asks herself. Really it doesn't matter what Jackie talks about, Cecilia would listen, her granddaughter's words fascinating, opening up other worlds.

Jackie is studying, though, and Cecilia doesn't want to interrupt her. She can wait until the end of the school day. It isn't that far away. She pushes off the car and hobbles to the end of the parking lot. She can't quite feel her legs anymore, or most of the rest of her body, but the sensation doesn't bother her. This end of the parking lot is unused and the snow is deep and drifting, but she pulls herself up as far as she can go, dropping her purse somewhere along the way to better keep her balance. At the top of the snowdrift, she pictures the pavement beneath and the map that is probably long gone by now. Standing in Texas. Hopscotching to Wisconsin. Splashing across the Great Lakes.

And that sky. Gray purple with the setting sun and the coming winter. Those billowy clouds racing across her line of vision. She strains to see past the clouds, to understand what comes next. Beside her a little girl hops, her purple scarf lifting in the wind. Maniac, Maniac, Maniac Magee. The girl turns and shields her eyes. Some days are like doors. Time collapses, expands. Potential pulses in her chest. Heat flickers at the edge of her skin, the edge of her eyes. The little girl reaches out her hand and patiently waits.

The Sadness of Spirits

The Sadness of Spirits

The spirits gather around the Ouija board. They never know which one of them will be called, but they are hopeful. They have messages, words of advice, theories on life that they have spent thousands of years perfecting. They are still working toward spiritual actualization, but that is a long process, often involving the silent voice of the Almighty whispering in their ears. The Almighty is not an easy entity to understand. "And then you will eat the lonely fruit of absolution," he seems to say. "And the prairie dogs will roost, and the buzz seals will sweep to the skies."

"What?" they reply. "What does that even mean?"

The Almighty tends not to repeat himself. He will share the secrets of the universe only once.

They could always reincarnate, get back to the earthly plane they know and love, which seems to be a pretty sweet deal until they remember all the pitfalls of being human: migraines, traffic jams, parking tickets, insane neighbors, long workweeks, tofu cooked by well-meaning vegetarian friends, newscasters in loud clothing, food poisoning, allergies, in-laws, Judge Judy, the entirety of adolescence, hormonal imbalances, foot pain, knee pain, the pain of being around fools, malls on Saturdays, not-so-flattering mirrors, hospitals, their own death.

Clearly, the better alternative is to stick it out on the spiritual plane.

They hover near the Ouija board even when it is not in use because they know that the second a human removes the board from its box, there will be a virtual stampede. Every spirit from the seven closest planes will come elbowing and kicking and pushing his or her way in, clamoring to be the one to speak. Some spirits go so far as to encircle the board with their energies, draping themselves around it in the only way they know how.

"Hey," the others say, "you can't do that."

"Yes, I can," the encircling spirit says and only clings tighter.

The spiritual plane is beautiful, but they have no qualms with leaving it to congregate in the closet of the Ouija board owner. Pterodactyl-sized butterflies and waving fields of poppies are only so enticing. They can watch only so many romantic sunsets and dance across the galaxy so many times before they grow bored. Instead, they wedge themselves between coats and shoes and shirts and wait. They vibrate at different intensities, each unique pattern signifying their spiritual development. They come from different planes, but their needs are the same. They vibrate together. They vibrate apart. They wait.

Finally, a human comes, a little boy about nine years old. He pulls the Ouija board down in the darkness—forbidden, no doubt, by his parents from using the board. He tucks it under his arm and tiptoes back to his room, and the spirits follow in droves. Back in the safety of the bedroom, he arranges the board on the floor with painstaking care. Then he rests his hands on the pointer, closes his eyes, and thinks of his question.

The spirits lean closer, waiting. One pushes another out of the way, and his vibration slows, a spiritual regression.

The boy flicks on his flashlight. He whispers, "Is anyone here?"

The spirits scramble—there are so many of them here—but the pointer is seized by a spirit of medium vibrational intensity who has been wrapped around the board for months. Carefully guiding the boy's pointer, she says, "Yes."

The boy draws back, looks down at the board as if he doesn't know what happened. Then he replaces his hands on the pointer and asks, "Who are you?"

The other spirits move closer. There are so many ways they might identify themselves: by previous names, as ghosts, as aliens, but the spirit brushes the others away and spells out *f-r-i-e-n-d*.

The boy mouths the word to himself. "If you're my friend," he says, "then what is my favorite food?"

The spirits exchange glances, their energies rising and falling rapidly. They are exposed to many ideas and emotions on their journey to spiritual actuality, but food is basically off their radar.

Spaghetti, someone volunteers.

Macaroni and cheese.

Rather than being wrong, the spirit with the pointer says nothing. The boy is quiet and then asks, "Are my parents going to die soon?"

He has no reason to think this other than the fact that he is nine and his parents are important and death seems large and terrible. The spirit could question him, ask him about the meaning of *soon*. Is soon tomorrow or ten years from now? And what exactly is death, but a trip to this new plane and time spent in his closet if they so choose?

She could also tell him that years are unimportant, that time coils and uncoils, and what matters are the events in between, the depth of each experience. She can give him specific dates and times, but it is his journey to figure this out, just as it is her journey to allow him to figure this out.

"What about my dog?" he asks.

Again, the spirit says nothing. The silence is deadening.

"Should I be afraid of death?" the boy asks, and he is a small, somber person squinting into a board, searching for an answer he can't have.

The spirit can't help herself. Even as her vibration slows, she wraps his hands in her energy, caresses him with her being as she would her own child—but the boy only falls back, feeling nothing but the bitter cold.

Uncle Rumpelstiltskin Will
Teach You to Dance

When he's not finagling babies, he is dancing. He dances where
no one can see him, behind the closed doors of his bathroom. Rising on tiptoe, spinning, spinning, he is a small man with good intentions. His hands brush the sink, the towel rack, the handle of
his door. The bathroom is really too small for his antics, but that
doesn't matter. He is concerned with the moment when he stops
and the world keeps moving.

He has been dancing and stopping, dancing and stopping for
as long as he can remember, and this is what he knows: the dizzy
moment that remains is everything.

He puts his hands to his face and closes his eyes. The air is
vibrating and the mirror is vibrating and the bathroom tiles are

vibrating, but when he peers closer through the darkness of closed eyes he sees atoms, strings playing a song, and that song is material: earth, air, water. If he concentrates hard enough, he can tune those strings, recreate creation.

There are other spaces, too. Spaces tucked and twisted within the strings, other worlds, but he can't reach those yet. They are tantalizingly close but just out of his grasp.

He knows this because he is intuitive—he can listen to what others won't hear—but he also knows this because he is empty and can't be filled. He is empty because his mother left him for plague and his father left him for plague and everywhere there are bodies destructing from the inside out, and what he needs to know, what he can't know, is why, and what happens next.

He peers into molecular fabrics and can change plastic to steel, glass to stone. He knows how to do this now, but what he doesn't know is how to root through the ground and recover carbon, hydrogen, oxygen and weave them back into a whole person.

The answer is there, though. He only has to be patient and listen.

His emptiness takes him to the bar. The world is still spinning, but it is a quiet hum against the band playing on the stage. He drinks an ale and orders another. He watches the bartender, the other patrons, eyes their drinks. If he concentrates enough, he can change what they are drinking—turn every glass to water, grape juice, Kool-Aid—and they would never know what hit them, but that would be a frivolous use of his skills. He considers himself a scientist even though no laboratory has ever hired him, no school has ever had the privilege of his insight. He is purely self-taught, a student of consciousness and quantum theory.

A woman sits down next to him. She doesn't know that he is both myth and mortal. She only knows that he is short.

The Sadness of Spirits

He considers changing the color of her hair or turning her purse into a rat, anything that will show her that the world is never safe, although he's not sure why he feels like she needs to know this lesson. He is considering other cruel ways to tease her when she turns to him and smiles. "This is a good song."

"It is," he says and suddenly wants to tell her how it appears to him: shivering atoms twisting like a snake. He wants to tell her how hypnotically that snake dances, how he wishes he could fall into its movements and be a part of it, although he's not sure he could get himself out again. There is all this to say and so much more, but what he says is, "Can I buy you a drink?"

She agrees, and he orders another ale. He has never wanted to share so much with someone before, except that he has, but it's been a while and maybe this time will be different. He asks her what her name is, and she asks the same. "Rumpelstiltskin," he says even though he's not supposed to give it away.

She laughs. "Does that mean you can spin straw into gold?"

"Yes," he says, his eyes all seriousness. "I can definitely do that."

And she moves closer, asks him to tell her more.

There have been babies and there will be more babies. In the past people believed that he ate them, but that was before he learned to be subtle. You don't want to draw too much attention to yourself when you're carting babies off to the woods.

He had to move to another continent to reestablish himself: America, the land of opportunity. He went about his life in an orderly and businesslike way. He courted women, struck deals, and traded firstborn children. When a woman—grief-stricken, weeping—tried to back out by saying, "But I know what your name is," he said, "I know it, too, and no, it's not a free pass." He currently has no children, but recently he had two and before that he had twelve.

It had been an especially tumultuous year and he found himself with more babies than he could handle, and so he rented a ground-floor office building, loaded it with cribs, and opened a preschool. He told his neighbors and his neighbors told friends and before he knew it twelve babies became fifteen and then twenty. There was so much crying, so many diapers.

He will never forget that year.

He dispersed those babies far and wide, wrapping them neatly in blankets and leaving them at fire halls and hospitals and, once, on the doorstep of a kindly old woman. Then he returned home, poured himself a tall whiskey, and drank in the silence.

He has his cravings, though. It is a hunger he cannot satiate, and so there will be more, many more babies in the future.

Daisy, the woman from the bar, comes to visit on a Sunday morning. She is bearing a bottle of champagne and flowers, yellow daffodils that make him think of his mother so long ago. He sets the flowers in the center of the dining room table so they catch the light of the sun and tells Daisy to take a seat. He is cooking omelets, flipping them expertly in the pan. They don't talk much, he isn't a talker, but he's aware of her presence behind him, the effect she has on the air, this day's particular song.

Loneliness is the price he pays for his abilities. He has seen his parents die and a brother and a sister and two wives and pets, so many pets. He misses them all and sometimes imagines he hears the patter of their feet around him, their bodies a breath passing by, a wave of warm love. By touching existence he has somehow extended his own, but this doesn't impress him.

Sometimes it occurs to him that he has done things all wrong. He was supposed to go to them, not try to draw them to him.

He finishes the omelets and brings them to the table. He sees the straw Daisy has placed beside her plate, but he doesn't let his

The Sadness of Spirits

disappointment show. "I was curious," she says. "If you don't mind showing me."

"Of course not." Outside the window, the sun is shining and it is just an ordinary day after all. There is no magic here.

After breakfast, he takes her to the bedroom and drags the old spinning wheel from the closet. It purrs softly as he pedals, and he takes the straw, feeds it along. He closes his eyes as he works, listens to the straw. He can feel it changing in his hands, stiffening, growing heavy, but he doesn't care. He's done this so many times before.

Daisy is ecstatic. Really. She can't believe her eyes. She takes the straw-turned-gold from him and dances around the room. He wants to catch her and command her to close her eyes, to listen to the vibrations, but who knows what she would do with his knowledge, and so he lets her go, studies her face, and tries to find something redemptive there, but all he sees is a woman who would give a baby for a few pieces of former straw.

"Thank you," she says, coming to him and kissing him on the cheek. "I've never believed in magic before, but now I feel like anything is possible."

Nothing is possible, but he only nods. If he concentrates on that smile, he might be able to feel for her. If he can get her to see beyond that golden straw, he just might fall in love, but he has his doubts. He's been here too many times before.

Insanity is repeating the same thing over and over again, expecting different results, and maybe he is insane, dancing alone in his bathroom, chanting his own name. Maybe he is crazy when he spins straw for love or when he dreams of the next baby he will bring home and place in his old oak crib. It will be Daisy's baby, perhaps. Or another baby. It doesn't matter.

What matters is that he will be changing diapers and tickling tiny feet and heating up bottles. He will make up stories to tell the neighbors: his sister's sudden trip to Europe, his cousin's need for informal foster care, and he will laugh good-naturedly about teething, tantrums, all the technicalities of having a young child.

And at night he will lift the baby from the crib and hold him or her close. "You're here with Uncle Rumpelstiltskin," he will say, and the baby will look past him. "Uncle Rumpelstiltskin will teach you to dance."

He will cradle the baby in the crook of his arm and think about the void the child came from and the adult he or she will become. If he can stare into the baby's eyes long enough, he might be able to locate the life beyond this life, those other worlds bent and wrapped around our own where his parents and wives and pets reside. If he is a good parent, he might earn this child's love and start a family.

These are just dreams, though, and dreams are not reality. Reality is nitrogen and oxygen and carbon and iron, and magic is what breathes life into them. He can listen and search, but the only breath he knows is the wind in winter, the rustle of autumn descending on leaves, and the babies he holds but can't comprehend. But maybe that's a start. A baby. A breath. An insatiable urge to dance.

The Key Maker and His Kin

The sky here has a way of rising up, up into mournful melodies, as does my mother, as do I. I don't know where the music comes from, only that it is organic, a product of heart and breath and mouth curving into shapes I can't control. "We are simply open," my mother told me once. "We absorb so much of what is around us."

There is slate-gray sky and moss-coated trees and darting shadows recording our every move. There is history and the way our history undoes us, chord by aching chord. I wish I could close myself off, but there is something within me that stretches and opens. And I sing. I sing for myself, and I sing for all the others. I am pure, pained voice.

This is the woman within me: I imagine her at her bedroom window, curtain pulled aside, staring at the night sky. There is no moon. There are no stars. Just emptiness waiting to swallow. The sky has already begun its haunted song, but she has yet to accept the reality of this place. She tells herself the songs are just her imagination, a product of her now-disturbed mind, and not the landscape trying to claim her piece by piece.

She rests her head on her hands, her dark hair drawn back over her shoulders, and plans her escape. There is a high fence that conceals this house, but where there is a fence, there is a key. The key could be anywhere. In a box with another key. In her husband's desk. On her husband's person.

Her husband is the key maker. He possesses all the keys and always knows just where to find her, how to fit the exact-sized key in the door and swing it open to reveal her.

She imagines her footsteps across the dewy grass, slipping her own stolen key into the gate, her two children in tow, a boy, a girl.

The gate will creak in the night. Its solidity will crack, and her husband will see it.

She begins again. There is a fence, and she can always dig, can always climb. Beyond the fence, there is a stream she can follow at least until daylight. There is a forest to get lost in, but her husband has dogs.

The surrounding landscape is a map she has done her best to memorize, and in her imagination she retreats back into the house, tries again. There is a way out. There has to be a way out.

This is me: I carry a key in my pocket and can't stop singing. It is an old key, rough around the edges, spotted with rust, lacking the smooth lines and symmetries of contemporary keys. The songs I sing are the songs of the sky, except they ache. People tell me they never heard a sad song until I came along, and I know they've never met my mother or my grandmother. They ask me where the sad songs come from, how someone so young can be so weary, and I tell them I don't know, but I do—or at least I've heard the stories.

The Sadness of Spirits

Unlike the woman within me, I know this is a haunted place. The world has somehow gathered its darkness in this very spot, and the air is heavy with foreboding over what has already happened, over what is still to come. I'm not afraid, though. I walk the forest paths and sing, and the trees lean close. They alone seem to understand I sing in registers that aren't mine: the voices of men and women and children.

They say he opened the door to reveal her one night, the woman within me. The door to her home. The door to a sitting room where she was playing the piano, singing her songs. The light from a candle caught her features. She had long black hair and green eyes. As did my mother. As do I. She may or may not have smiled. She may or may not have followed him willingly.

There are two details I know about the key maker: he was the master of many keys, and not all of his keys were material.

He could charm and coerce. He could push, prod, and force.

He had the key to everything, but he underestimated the woman within me.

My song marks me mysterious, even to myself. I watch others smiling, talking with each other and laughing, and I wonder if there is a way in. If I could only look them over long enough, I might find a mechanism to unlock them, to step inside. If I could understand the strange gears of happiness, I might be able to discover it in myself.

"You have such an intensity about you," people say. "Didn't your mother ever teach you to smile?"

My mother taught me to walk these forest paths, to keep our secrets. She taught me about spirits and the way they can claim the body for their own. She taught me the many stories that circulate in this place and how they pertain to us.

They are our stories, perpetuated by others.

I want to slip into their minds, peer through their eyes, try to find a way out. I don't care if in the process of doing this I tear their minds apart.

I want to understand how they see me, if only to change the way I see myself.

There is nothing more witchlike than my hair, so shiny and dark. There is nothing more frightening than understanding I am just as much the key maker as I am his victim.

When I turned fifteen, my mother pressed a key into my hand and told me to keep it. There was no story because the stories had all been told. There was no story because there was no narrative that could be understood for certain.

We were sitting in my bedroom, and the dim light fell through the curtain. Beyond was the yard and the border where there used to be a fence. Beyond that the forest, dense enough to make a woman feel like she could disappear, not so dense as to ensure she wouldn't be found.

"My mother gave this to me," was all my own mother said. "And now I'm entrusting it to you. It's a part of our history. We have to be sure we never forget."

I held the key in my hand, feeling the rust flake off into the creases of my palm. In that moment I understood that no matter where I went, I wouldn't be able to escape because I would always carry that key. I would always have it even if I accidentally lost it, even if I buried it deep beneath the soil in an attempt to forget.

They say the woman within me had wandering fingers. They would slip along fresh apples, past the glistening beads of bracelets and necklaces before thrusting them into her bag. The shop owners would look at her with sympathy before calling the police and requesting that she be taken to jail. The authorities were always gentle with her. They were always kind.

The Sadness of Spirits

The eight-by-eight cell with its single barred window represented peace to her, and everyone knew it.

Sometimes she stayed for as little as an hour, but sometimes for as long as a day, but the key maker always came. If he didn't possess the key to her cell, he could make one. If her cell was well guarded, he could wield the key of his influence, his constant charm and authority.

Back at home, she sat at the window and studied the landscape. Yard to fence to the forest beyond. There had to be a route she hadn't thought of, another alternative that would lead to freedom, but she could never find a way.

I walk the forest paths, turning this way and that, singing, and I sense that someone is with me. A girl a couple of years younger is following me, listening to the sound of my voice. At first I think it is just a coincidence—she is wandering as I am wandering—but I don't know why she would want to wander here. She appears the next day and the day after. I wonder if she has friends, if she is here on a dare. I try to lose her by slipping through heavy bramble, past the shadows of the tallest trees, but she always finds me.

One afternoon I stop and confront her. "You've been following me," I say. "I want to know why."

I'm expecting the usual request to hear a song or questions about why I'm so sad, but she only says, "I noticed you come out here a lot and I wondered why."

"I'm just walking."

"I know."

"Don't you wonder why I'm walking?"

"It's very peaceful here. That makes sense to me."

I turn away from her then, but when she is waiting for me at the forest path the following day I allow her to come along. And I allow her to come the next day and the day after that until it begins to seem we are something like friends.

This is the part we often forget: there were also two children, a boy and a girl. They watched in fear as the key maker raged through their house, raised his fists against their mother.

They were taught that children should be seen and not heard. They didn't utter a word of protest when their mother told them to be quiet, to stop crying. They didn't ask questions when their mother told them to pack their bags with a few pairs of clothes, a book, their favorite toys, and to hide those bags under their beds.

They were told they were taking a trip.

They were told they were going to a better place, which is perhaps where these stories always begin.

"What does it feel like," the girl asks me, "to sing in the way that you do?" Her name is Caroline, and I appreciate the slow, halting way she asks me questions, as if she understands that not all stories are communal.

"It's singing," I say. "I wouldn't say it's any different."

That's a lie, but I don't know how else to explain it to her or even if I should. Some people talk about the muse as if it's some sort of divine being that comes down from above, but my songs come from somewhere deep inside me, somewhere so deep it's as if it isn't even me at all. The songs come and there is nothing I can do to stop them. I can't think. I can't move. I can't control my lips as they open and close to form the notes that really aren't mine.

"I guess you could say it's like a wave," I say finally. "The music comes and washes over me. It has nothing to do with who I am."

She nods, and I imagine I see a trace of skepticism, a smirk playing on the corner of her lips, but perhaps I've been conditioned to expect that reaction. I see only what I think I should see.

"I brought some cookies," I say because I want to please this newfound friend. "Let's find a place to sit down and eat them."

She smiles and gestures toward a clearing, and this time I know her expression is true.

I hold the key in my hand sometimes. I don't know if it's the key to unlock the bedroom door or the key to unlock the gate. And I will never know because the fence is gone and our doors no longer have locks.

The fence is gone, but somehow I am still here, as is my mother, as is the woman within me.

"What is it like to be a part of the town legend?" Caroline asks me. "Are you sometimes afraid of the ghosts?"

"I don't believe in ghosts," I say. "No rational person would."

"I heard there's a key," she says. "Have you ever seen it?"

"Have you ever thought about running away?" I ask. I peer into the distance, but all I really see are trees.

"No," she says. "Have you?"

"All the time," I tell her. "I think about it all the time."

This is where the story breaks down. The woman within me was looking for a way out, and she found it in the form of a merchant who brought his cart to the house three times a week. The plan was simple: stow the children in the back and ride away into the next town and then the next until she and the kids were somewhere different, somewhere safe.

Or she dug a hole under the fence. She made it bigger day after day, which sounds easy enough, but it involved furtive trips to the shed for the shovel and only enough time for a few shovelfuls to be moved a day. She transferred the soil to the garden or to the perpetual pile of grass clippings the gardener kept. She covered the hole with tree branches or a carefully created sheet of grass. Really, she used anything she could find.

Or she found a key and let herself out one day. Forgot the tell-tale creak of the gate, the way her husband might hear.

Or she gave up entirely, waited in her room until he came for her, unlocked the door.

A person can break down, they say. It's possible that by the end she simply stopped trying.

I sing as I walk through the woods, Caroline by my side. She is quiet when I sing, listening to the sound of my voice or perhaps to the sound of her own busy thoughts. I don't mean to ignore her, but when the music comes it is insistent, filled with note after note of longing and melancholy.

Sometimes I catch her watching me out of the corner of my eye, and she is smiling. She is trying not to laugh, and I wonder if she is that happy or if there is something I simply don't understand.

"Do you think it would help you," she asks one day, "to share some of what you know?"

"There's nothing to know," I say, and then I hesitate. My hand goes to my chest where a key is hidden beneath my shirt. I know I shouldn't share it with anyone, but the whole awful loneliness of my past presses down on me, and I unhook my necklace, hand the key over.

They say he found the woman within me in the woods or the next town or in the bedroom where she waited beside the billowing curtains. He dragged her, hands in her shiny hair, to the yard between fence and the house. He brought the kids, too. A boy and a girl.

There was a knife or a gun or a machete the gardener used to maintain the yard.

They ran or didn't run, tried to protect themselves or understood that it was futile.

Their screams curled into the air, animal-like, scorched with betrayal and fear. It was nothing you would ever want to hear. At least this one detail everyone can agree on.

Caroline takes the key and grips it tight. "I knew there was a key," she whispers. "Everyone said it was just a story, but I knew." She slips it in her pocket, and my heart stops in my chest. "You're so gullible," she says. "You should have known I only wanted the key."

I don't know what to say. I can hardly breathe. A song would serve me well now, a high and angry song that would shake her to the core, but I am emptied of music.

"I don't know what makes you think you're so special anyway," she says. "Look at you. Always singing and acting so dramatic. We all have problems. So what?"

Her voice is a sneer, and as I stand, a small and shaken version of myself with no words of my own, she turns and walks away, my key tucked safely in her pocket.

This is where my family comes in: the key maker took another wife, a woman who had long dark hair and green eyes, as did my mother, as did I. He must have seen the resemblance but thought nothing of it. The new wife came from a distant town and knew nothing of the murders until the people around her began to talk.

There were whispers, snippets of fact and story that came together to create a disorienting whole. The new wife could choose to believe or choose not to believe, but believing had its price.

They say she went for long walks at night, through the garden, along the perimeter of the fence, back and forth across the roof of the house, where the moon caught her hair and cast her in dark shadows. As she walked she sang in an unearthly voice. She sang like a woman possessed by troubled spirits. She sang like someone touched by the deaths of a woman and two children.

Her voice was my voice, haunted by the violence around her, frightened by her own unexpected complicity in it.

I wanted to chase Caroline, slap her hard across the face in the way my mother slapped me as a child, and reach into her pocket to collect the key, but I let her go. I felt there was nothing else to do.

Instead I sit at my bedroom window, watching the night sky, feeling the absent weight where the key should be. I think about DNA, those winding strands of ourselves that are dictated to us by the people who came before. The key maker and his wrath. The key maker and his talent for manipulation, the opening of every locked door.

Then I think about my great-great-grandmother standing on the roof of our house, her voice swelling in the moonlit air. It may not have been pure sorrow she was singing of; it may have been her attempt to put the broken pieces back together. The only narrative is the one we create. Our history is only part of the picture.

Pushing back the curtain, I clear my throat and begin to hum, quietly at first and then louder and clearer. This time I am not waiting for that unknown source within me. I am following my own lead. I am singing my own song, and where it takes me is breathtaking and bold, a haunted place where only I can go.

The Sadness of Spirits

Aimee Pogson teaches creative writing at Penn State Erie, the Behrend College, where she also serves as coeditor of *Lake Effect*. She received her MFA from Bowling Green State University.